Fragile Travelers

Jovanka Živanović

FRAGILE TRAVELERS

A Novel

Translated by Jovanka Kalaba

DALKEY ARCHIVE PRESS

First published in Serbian as *Putnici od stakla* by Geopoetika in 2008.

Library of Congress Cataloging-in-Publication Data

Names: Živanović, Jovanka, 1959- author. | Kalaba, Jovanka, translator.
Title: Fragile travelers / Jovanka Zivanovic ; translated by Jovanka Kalaba.
Other titles: Putnici od stakla. English
Description: First edition. | Victoria, TX : Dalkey Archive Press, 2016.
Identifiers: LCCN 2016006313 | ISBN 9781943150038 (pbk. : acid-free paper)
Classification: LCC PG1420.36.I935 P8813 2016 | DDC 891.8/236--dc23
LC record available at https://lccn.loc.gov/2016006313

Partially funded by the Illinois Arts Council, a state agency.
This translation has been published with the financial support of the Republic of Serbia Ministry of Culture and Information.

www.dalkeyarchive.com
Victoria, TX / McLean, IL / London / Dublin

Dalkey Archive Press publications are, in part, made possible through the support of the University of Houston-Victoria and its programs in creative writing, publishing, and translation.

Cover: Art by Eric Longfellow

Printed on permanent/durable acid-free paper

Translator's Preface

I came across this book in 2008, the same year it came out. It received negligible media coverage upon publication, and I, being engaged in various activities that paid my bills in those days and none of them having anything to do with literature or publishing, hadn't heard anything about it. At the time I was renting a small courtyard flatlet in downtown Belgrade, and my landlady was working part-time as a cleaning lady in the offices of Geopoetika, a well-known publishing house. Normally she'd come to collect the rent at the end of every month. One time she couldn't, so she asked me to come to Geopoetika's offices one Thursday evening after working hours. She was going about her business when I arrived, so she told me to take a seat and wait until she finished. The chair was next to a pile of books strewn carelessly on the floor. And so I picked one, out of many, to pass the time. It was *Putnici od stakla*, the original version of *Fragile Travelers*. I had just enough time to read the first chapter—five minutes or so. Then my landlady came, we exchanged a few words, I gave her the money, and I left.

The chapter that I'd read made quite an impression on me, but at that point I didn't have time to read the whole book. Years passed; at various times I'd forget the title, then the author's name, or both, and then I'd get scared that I'd forget about it completely and wouldn't be able to find it one day when I finally found time and it mattered. So I'd search for it on the Internet and make notes, which I'd then lose, over and over again, until

2014 and the Applied Literary Translation Program organized in Dublin by Dalkey Archive Press and the University of Illinois for aspiring literary translators, for which I was supposed to find a novel to translate. I'd managed to find the time to read some other books in the interim, and they weren't bad, but ironically, none of them made as strong an impression as that one chapter of *Putnici od stakla*. I finally gave it a chance, and the decision was easy: my translation project was going to be *Putnici od stakla*.

The translation of this book proved to be quite a challenge. A marvelous read as it was, the novel featured several thematic and interpretive layers. These allowed it to be read either as an engaging mystery story of forbidden love between two small-town acquaintances, Emilija and Petar, or as a piece of metaphysical fiction about the modern condition of man and his spiritual and emotional growth—a fictional tackling of philosophical and religious questions. The story is told almost entirely in the alternating voices of the two main protagonists, while the introduction, conclusion, and several other chapters are presented by an omniscient narrator. Although much of the story's action takes place in the often surreal settings of Emilija's dreams, where "the strangest of plots unfolded, featuring incongruous characters in unlikely settings," the narrator in the original is easily recognized from the forms of the verbs, adjectives, numbers, etc. of the Serbian language which distinguish grammatical gender. For example, the first sentence of Chapter 2, narrated by the female protagonist, opens with the sentence: "Dlanovima sam stisla naspramne nadlaktice," in which "sam stisla" is the feminine form of the past tense of the verb "stisnuti," meaning "I (a woman) hugged myself." (The masculine would be "sam stisnuo.") The original's long and complex sentences, replete with powerful imagery, intertextual allusions, and symbolism, as well as inversions, metaphors and personifications, acquire a tone of both epic force and lyrical poignancy, and yet can be playful and light when drawing on postmodern devices and strategies such as metafiction, irony, and parody.

The original text brims with highly idiosyncratic figurative language, especially when it comes to what might be called the literalization of metaphors. The imagery of the novel rests on the metaphors that are reduced to their literal meaning and further developed in such a way as to create a ludic or surreal effect. In Chapter 3, the novel literalizes the Serbian expression "pustiti mozak na otavu," which quite literally means "to put your brain out to pasture"—or, figuratively, to relax. The main protagonist's brain pleads with him to be allowed to run loose for a while, which leads to the comical and nonsensical literalization of the metaphor:

> My brain was turning back and forth in the grass, then did a whirling somersault followed by a gracious axel, all sorts of miraculous stunts and acrobatics while shouting in exaltation. It's nice to make a brain feel joyful, even if it's one's own brain, I thought—although, quite paradoxically, with the brain running loose, I actually had nothing to think *with* at that point.

There is another example of this kind of use of metaphor in Chapter 7. The main protagonist, feeling guilty about thinking about another woman, sets off on an imaginary swimming adventure down the Morava and Danube rivers, and thereby goes through an act of ritual purification trying to "wash away his sins." The meaning of the whole chapter rests on the phrase "neće te oprati ni Dunav ni Sava," the literal translation of which would be "neither the Danube nor the Sava will clean you," an expression commonly used in Serbian to convey the speaker's doubt about someone's ability to *remove the moral stain* of an immoral act.

This translation seeks to convey the best qualities of the

original by placing the emphasis on the atmosphere created by the book's nuances and complexities—rather than by translating the nuances and complexities themselves—so as to make the English version of *Putnici od stakla* a pleasurable, page-turning read.

To Ciarán Doyle, my Dublin landlord in 2014 and now my friend, I am especially indebted for his kindness and the invaluable help that he, as a native English speaker and a literary enthusiast, gave me while I was working on and later revising the translation.

Jovanka Kalaba
Belgrade, Serbia
December 2015

Fragile Travelers

Chapter 1
Coffee Lovers Move in Mysterious Ways

GIVEN HOW DEFTLY he could bounce the coffee can in his hand, he didn't have to take off the lid to know that it was empty. He realized that if he wanted coffee, he would have to run down to the kiosk on the ground floor of his building. Such occurrences of his being absent from the apartment, unplanned for and only for a short while, didn't require much clothing, so Petar, without closing the door behind him, dashed out of the apartment foyer in his slippers. The water he'd left boiling on the gas burner had no other option but to wait. It waited until the last drop, and when it evaporated, the water, logically enough, ceased to be aware of itself and therefore had no means to keep on waiting any longer. And even if it had been able to, there wouldn't have been anyone to wait for, because Petar wasn't coming back. Ten days had passed since he left the apartment, and he was now considered a missing person. The disappearance had been reported to the police that same day. The case stalled, however, at the level of a police promise that something would be done, and many days had now passed without any progress.

How was the disappearance discovered? Who discovered and then reported it? What had happened in the apartment? Bearing in mind that the lit burner had been flirting openly with an extremely dangerous situation and had thus provided the required thrilling suspense, no one really knew for sure. Two options were considered. Those who get a kick out of crime

3

stories claimed that the fire in the apartment had burned through the ceiling to the upstairs neighbor's carpet, that the flames gnawed at the massive legs of his oak dining table, thus forcing the unfortunate man to regress several centuries and eat on his knees with his elbows on a low table. The evidence indicated that it hadn't been an electrical fault or an act of arson, and that one of the apartment's occupants had been there shortly before the tragedy, but which one? The mystery was easily resolved when Mrs. Anđelija Naumov, Petar's wife, appeared at the scene of the fire. From the terrified expression on her face, her hair standing on end, it became clear that she wasn't the one.

She'd just come back from a seminar organized by a well-respected, globally renowned insurance company where she had recently secured herself a job. She'd learned how to convince people that there was nothing more urgent or more important than insurance. She'd absorbed with unflinching single-mindedness how to put pressure on her clients, empty their pockets, and strip them of their very last cent. Her clients had to realize that, because things had gotten serious, they had to deny themselves everything; their children wouldn't become people of character unless they went through some tough times—it was absurd to grant every teenage wish—and so, money had to be more smartly invested . . . And everything would eventually be paid off; if not earlier, then on the final journey to the last stop—in one's own luxury-brand funeral coach.

She'd attended lectures on all that, then gone for long walks and enjoyed her evenings listening to the orchestra playing at the foot of the hotel patio. All those fresh and beautiful memories on one side, and now, on the other, the charred remains in front of her eyes—a turn of events that could kill her on the spot. And she would die, God have mercy on her, without her husband. She couldn't live without him, nor did she want to, but first she had to find him. She was there, and he, undoubtedly, was there too, in the form of ashes. Yes, he always used to say that he wanted to be cremated (*you'll get what you want, ah, you impossible man!*), but not like this—with no plan, no meaning. And how was she supposed to separate Petar's ashes from the pile, how was she supposed to know that those were his remains and not, for example, those of the latest "Dunlop" sports bag? Someone suggested that they should clean the narrowest area around the jawbones and teeth, they could make no mistake about that—but there were no teeth, there were no bones, there was nothing of Petar there. The acknowledgement that her husband wasn't there, at least in the form of ashes, completely devastated Mrs. Naumov. If he wasn't there *for her*, then he was dead; she couldn't accept any other option. And now what?! Oh, wretched me, the grieving woman wailed while descending into the abyss of a widow's fate.

The fact that none of Petar Naumov's physical remains were found suited well those who speculated upon a different option for the story and saw this entangled situation with a different eye. Since they were shocked by the morbidity of the thorough search for Petar Naumov's ashes in the previous paragraph, they completely dismissed the possibility of fire. According to them, the apartment was intact because the stove had run out of gas just in time. The moment the red-hot bottom of the coffee pot had started to crackle and discharge enamel flakes, the flame began to weaken, and soon it was completely gone. This view of the situation was approved rather enthusiastically by the upstairs neighbor who, without hiding his relief, was sitting like a normal human being at his oak table again. The only thing that both sides agreed upon was the last sentence, and therefore it was used in the latter side's closing word as well: And now what?! Oh, wretched me, the grieving woman wailed while descending into the abyss of a widow's fate.

The Naumovs led a secluded life, sticking pretty much to themselves, and not much was known about them, which was enough to keep a number of kidnapping versions open. A political kidnapping hadn't been ruled out, although motives of a financial nature were holding on too. The most persistent options, however, were favored by the readers of *The Third Eye*[1] and avid collectors of articles and stories on mysteries and paranormal occurrences, those who couldn't but see the hand of a UFO in this whole predicament. They spent sleepless nights filled with anxiety and impatience in enthusiastic anticipation of the return of the fortunate man, hoping to hear revelatory news from the abductee himself.

Even if any of the above-mentioned theories were in fact true, they couldn't have traveled, even as rumors, to the place where Petar actually ended up. Even if they had, that wouldn't be important. On his way to buy some coffee, Petar ended up in a woman's dream—and got stuck there.

Although modern-day investigative techniques are superior, almost faultless, they're still powerless when it comes to dreams, so when questions such as *who travels to whom? when?* and *why?* pop up, they're simply dismissed without a word and with a helpless shrug of the shoulders. Dreamers mostly keep quiet about their adventures, unless they're on a psychiatrist's sofa; there aren't any other sources of information. And so dreams, often so much fuller than life itself, remain closed and unused in the darkness, never to be interpreted, which is a shame. They're often so torturous and dense that mornings find it hard to open the terrified eyes of so many unfortunate souls.

This story, too, would have reached a dead end, just like the inquest, had Petar Naumov and Emilija Savić not left written records about their unusual experience.

---

1. A Serbian magazine on paranormal phenomena.

Chapter 2
Ema Savić's Welcoming Dreams—A Woman's Actual or Parallel Life

I HUGGED MYSELF, holding on like that because there was nothing to lean on, or at least nothing I could see. Either it was dark outside or I was in a place that was out of the sun's reach. It was cold and damp; large, heavy drops of water were falling from somewhere. I was shaking, afraid. I wished I was able to bend my knees and crouch, bury my head so that I could find some comfort in the warmth of my breath. I wished, but I couldn't, knowing that nothing good would come of it. As long as I was standing, as long as I was on my two feet, there was hope that I would move forward . . .

Had my sight been sharpened by the darkness or had I just seen some light? I wasn't sure, but I saw it. Dim and faint, a whitish beam of light lured me towards what I guessed was the exit of a dark cave. I barely succeeded in ungluing my feet from the ground. I made the first unsteady step, then the second, the third, when my elbows started rubbing against a cold, moist stone ledge. Despite being overcome with fear, I could sense clearly that the tunnel was narrowing, the exit was far away . . . Intense pain in my temples forced my hands to my forehead, only for them to close around something that felt like an enormous wreath of tightly plaited thorns. If I continued forward, the wreath would start tightening around my head, and that would be the end of me. With each step, the thorns

7

would dig deeper into my heavy-throbbing temples; they'd drill the bone and then rest there in the softness of the hot, dead cerebrum. God help me, I can't do it, the burden is too heavy!—I managed to cry out the most honest of sobs, the only kind that God actually hears.

Blood was on my cheeks, and with great effort I moved forward slowly. Still, each successive step I made was quicker and lighter than the one before, because I knew—my savior was there. The pounding in my chest had prevented me from noticing the moment when he'd appeared, but the feeling of relief that sank in testified of his soothing presence. I sensed him following me one step at a time, gently touching my left side. He was doing it very lightly and only because he had to, since there was no other way to help me. He put his hands on the wreath and pulled it backwards, making it possible for me to pass through the narrow exit of the cave. You can do it, just hold on—I felt rather than heard the whisper behind my left ear. I was enduring a small pain to avoid a larger one, something unbearable, maybe deadly. My forehead was pulsing with thin, interrupted spurts, the quantity insufficient for the life itself to spill out. A few drops of blood ran down an unbuttoned cuff of Petar Naumov's shirt.

* * *

If anybody asked me how long I'd known Petar Naumov and what had made our lives intersect so strangely in the first place, I'd become ashamed and confused, knowing how innocent Petar was in the whole matter. I couldn't tell where reality ended and dreams began, and I couldn't speak of one realm and not betray the other. The thin dividing line between the two represented the beginning and the end of the same circle—a curved trajectory, hardly visible, almost unreal. Both the starting and the finishing point of that trajectory was Petar's face, starting as just another person I'd recognize in the streets of my hometown and say hello to, and finishing with that same face transformed into a guardian angel—a savior. I could see the sketch of that trajectory as if it were drawn on the back of my hand, so clear, and yet—it revealed nothing. How he had found himself passing from one point to the other was a secret to me. I guessed that it had to remain so. Miracles are not something that ordinary people can easily fathom, and playing with supernatural experiences is as dangerous as tightrope walking without a safety net. So, suspecting that any further curiosity on my part could be dangerous for both of us, I decided to let it go.

I was having all sorts of *cross-genre* dreams and nightmares at that time. They flashed through my mind in still frames; the strangest of plots unfolded, featuring incongruous characters in unlikely settings. Admittedly there had been delicious, carnal dreams too, but they were quite rare. One could say that erotic dreams were completely unworthy of a woman who, judging by the temptations she usually felt in her sleep, may as well have aspired to become a saint! Still, no one is as perfect as our Lord . . . Such thoughts gave me comfort. Innocent dreams, on the other hand, were more frequent. Tormenting and ascetic, these were the ones that Petar Naumov haunted. Although uninvited, he would come as support, as some kind of spiritual stimulant, as the stronger part of me—a man who could lift a burden heavier than himself without even being aware of it.

I didn't consider myself to be special, nor did I believe that I was the only one who had come to see the infinitude of the spiritual world as a safe haven. But this world was mine, just the way it was. It was from this world that I drew the strength to make the worldly days go by as painlessly as possible. As far as my savior was concerned, I was immensely grateful to him. He was to be mentioned in my prayers. In most cases I am far too thankful when I shouldn't be: to a hairdresser for a bad hairdo, to a dressmaker for a crooked seam, to an impolite shop assistant or a clerk. However, I was afraid to be thankful to Petar. As there was no way to be sure whether any of this was true, I was scared of being mistakenly grateful to the man and creating a completely wrong image of my own foolish self. That was why we simply got on with our lives without a word, each going down a separate path.

However, paths have a peculiar way of crossing one another, so we would meet from time to time and even exchange a few words. There was nothing strange about it, given that we came from the same town and knew each other from get-togethers attended by lots of people, where we'd make small talk on the usual superficial topics . . . and that was all. It could be that a desire for longer and deeper conversation had been conceived in that small talk, that deep down, beneath the surfaces, in some subliminal place, a soul recognized a soul—it could be . . . and yet not necessarily.

After the dream in which he'd appeared for the first time, I stood for quite a while feeling utterly dazed, not as much by the content of the dream (which was intriguing enough for me to dwell on for at least a half hour) as by Petar's presence in it. Not before three or four dreams did I actually recognize who he was. He kept away; he hid in dark corners—it was important to him not to be exposed, as if he were Hermes. But at one moment, as I was running from a catastrophic natural disaster which included a simultaneous tsunami, tornado, and earthquake, completely overcome with panic, I turned my head abruptly and saw his face.

There was no other way to see this whole thing other than as a figment of my imagination; still, with my body and soul I refused to disregard it as irrelevant. As for Petar, I sensed that he knew nothing of his heroic deeds. And what did I really know about him? Not much: that he was a handsome, well-thought-of man with dark hair, dark eyes, and a fair complexion. He was educated, had good manners, and was levelheaded in the way he spoke and acted—neither too relaxed nor stiff. He was a family man without a stain, an architect by profession with extraordinary analytical abilities. I admired everything about him because of my idiotic enthusiasm for people who could do everything that I couldn't: pilots, parachutists, divers, surgeons, high-rise window washers, professional prostitutes, jugglers, and practitioners of other marvelous crafts. In a word, *happy was the mother who had him*. However, spiritual spheres might have been entirely foreign to him, and upon hearing all this he might have said: God, save me from lunatics. Even if it was so, I wouldn't take back a single word I'd just said.

Chapter 3
Salvation as a Divine Idea and the Danger of Personifying It

After Ema went out through the opening I remained inside the cave for a while, concealed by the stone ledge. I hoped she hadn't seen me. The idea of salvation as an act of mercy comes from higher authorities and is beyond our understanding, and therefore personifying it or attributing it to anyone's face (in this case mine) could be a dangerous thing. Those blessed by God's mercy shouldn't feel indebted to any earthly creature, and if, by any unfortunate accident, Ema had seen me when she turned, such unworthy gratitude couldn't be avoided.

Looking at my watch made me nervous. I refused to believe that it was working properly. I was waiting for a miracle to make the hands go backwards, but none was granted to me; the watch persisted in claiming that it was eight o'clock, which meant that I was late for work yet again. I knew what my tardiness meant in this particular case. I'd been admonished and warned several times before, and now I was on probation, so to speak. No longer was a good, innocent face enough, nor were the awards bestowed on me for my most successful architectural projects. The privatization of the project bureau where I worked meant that my relaxed attitude towards time and my theories about the productive utilization of working hours had become entirely out of place—even liable to incur discipline. In vain had I argued that it was more honest to read the newspapers and have my first coffee at home. That way, when I arrived at the office, I would apply myself to work immediately and do more in three hours than someone else would in nine. Every time I'd give a sermon of this kind, my boss would smugly remind me of the embarrassing incident at the beginning of my (why be modest about it?) stellar career.

It was three days before the unveiling of my third solo design—a memorial on a steep slope on the outskirts of town. The workers employed on the project started submitting requests to be allowed to go and attend "the Guča Trumpet." What's that? I asked a perfectly legitimate question for a newcomer, only recently settled in town. A big trumpet festival, a crazy time, they said, and I could see that they were really dying to go. They shifted nervously from one leg to the other and wrung their hands, fearing that I wouldn't allow them. They *were* definitely going—there was no question about it, but they needed my blessing so that they wouldn't end up out of a job. And they got it. They promised they would work until they dropped in the days to come and that the deadline would be met, assuring me that any concern on my part was utterly uncalled-for. Everything was a question of organization and motivation, they explained—the first, of course, totally conditioned by the latter.

After they left, I circled around the monument and examined it, feeling proud. My accomplishment was really something to *take my hat off to.* And I did, and then, given that the sun was high in the sky already, other pieces of clothing as well. I hadn't spent much time in the sun that summer due to overwork, so, piece by piece, I started exposing my young white body to its warmth. I took off my shoes, then my T-shirt. I looked around me—not a living soul was anywhere near, so my pants went down too. I found myself a cozy sunny spot and lay down. Alone for some time now, I stared into the deep blue, feeling tranquil. I emptied my head, placed it on my palms and stopped thinking. In such a mental vacuum I could almost hear my brain plead with me: come on Petar, let me run loose for a while! It won't take long, just to sweat a little bit, release all the poison. You know I won't be any good to you if I keep on like this . . . The impassioned animal succeeded in persuading me, and so I let it run loose; I would for sure have regretted it if I hadn't. Such joy, such euphoria . . . ! My brain was turning back and forth in the grass, then it did a whirling somersault followed by a gracious axel, all sorts of miraculous stunts and acrobatics while shouting in exaltation. It's nice to make a brain feel joyful, even if it's one's own brain, I thought—although, quite paradoxically, with the brain running loose, I actually had nothing to think *with* at that point.

A sensation of drowsiness took hold of me and I surrendered without thinking twice or feeling any discomfort. I didn't know how much time I'd spent sleeping but I knew how I was awoken—violently, as if by a heart attack. The brain, all flustered and petrified by something, rushed back to its place with such force that I came within a whisker of not ever getting up. Get up, it breathed heavily from its cortex, get up Petar, some people are coming! I've seen government plates on their cars . . . Hurry up, you good-for-nothing, get dressed! In a second I was on my feet, but I had no time to dress. I managed somehow to grab my work coat and wrap my nude body into it as fast as I could. The delegation, consisting of my university professor, a widely acclaimed architectural guru, and a couple of well-known politicians, were standing very close. The group dealt with the situation wisely by stopping and remaining at a safe distance. I didn't need a mirror to know that, with my bare legs and chest and the casually worn work coat whose tails I'd crossed over my stomach, I looked like a local maniac that jumps out of hedges and thickets and scares lonely women strolling around. Obviously, I wasn't a maniac, and the gentlemen weren't women strolling around, but the logical follow-up of this image could very likely be one of me with the coat open and my phallus exposed like a statue of an ancient hero.

To make a long story short, it all ended well. My monument stood alongside the best of its kind in the world. And now, if this lateness got me fired, it would be quite fair, because here I was, dwelling on tarnished memories from my biography, and also, where? In a dark and damp cave from Emilija Savić's dream. At least I was sure that she had gotten away by now and that it was completely safe for me to exit.

Snowdrifts had piled up at the entrance of the cave. Dazed by the whiteness, I stood for a while like a blind man, trying to sniff out my current position in order to determine which way to go next. I looked cautiously at the ground, hesitating for a moment, but then I allowed my eyes to roam. I saw Ema's shallow trail, almost completely covered with the snow layering over it. I started following the trail like a sleepwalker. The straight line consisting of evenly spaced steps indicated the walker's confidence and conviction that the chosen path was the right one. However, as things are usually deceptive, that impression didn't last for long. The trail thinned out and became skewed, turned into haze and illusion, because . . . after a few meters I saw the edge of the cliff. There was nothing beyond it except an abyss. A dark premonition came over me suddenly. Premonitions are there to warn in advance—that's what they do. In this particular case, however, there was no time, and I found myself terrified and frozen to the bone, on the very edge of the cliff. While I was mustering the courage to look down, my eyes squinted cowardly under the eyebrows. They wouldn't look into the abyss, and chose to stare straight ahead, into the distance. No! It couldn't be . . . I refused to believe the image in front of me; not even in dreams could such things be seen. I blinked three times, and each time the same still frame appeared before my eyes. Like a butterfly pinned to a board in a display case, Ema was suspended over the abyss, pressed against a precipice that dropped down vertically, sharply, straight as an arrow. She floated in the air hesitantly, as if unsure whether to come down to earth or not, resembling a creature that had fallen from another world.

Having no other choice, I went towards her. I didn't intend to, it was an impulse, as natural as breathing. Only later, after a lot of dreaming, did I succeed in defining it. I realized that if a man's nature (even if that man be me) is Samaritan, then an act of compassion is never by conscious decision but by natural reflex.

Chapter 4
Those Who Miss the Signposts in Real Life Can Only Look for Them in Dreams

THE END OF my dreaming ordeal was nowhere in sight. I was put to yet another endurance test without even a moment to recover from the previous dream. This time, however, the test was clearly impossible to pass. Even if the whole thing was for my own good, whoever was out there tempting me had overestimated my strength.

I hovered, suspended over the abyss, held up only by some long spikes driven through my feet and palms, and yet they seemed as if they were growing out of the thick layer of snow on the ledge. My body was growing weaker and I couldn't keep my head up; I felt irresistibly drawn to the bottomless pit below. Although I was out of my mind with fear, I knew that I was in no physical danger, and that if I didn't pull through this time, I would suffer a completely different kind of fall.

I was looking at the endless blue space below me. I wanted to raise my head and send a prayer from my lips towards the sky, but there was no need for that because—I realized—*the sky was below me* as well. But people cling to their preconceptions tenaciously and have a hard time breaking a habit of seeing things as they always do—even if it's just a piece, not more than a shard of broken sky, it counts only if it's *above*. And so my crazy curiosity prevailed, like a desperate soul's masochistic need to take a last look at the abandoned path before being swallowed up.

I raised my head and began to observe. My gaze glided deftly across the glittering snow, then rested on what appeared to be a sunlit, grassy plateau enclosed by the sky. All of a sudden, I felt someone propelling me towards it, propping my numb legs from below, imbuing them with life and thawing the frozen blood in my veins. I felt my strength coming back from the darkness of anxiety. My blood, red and vigorous, flowed forcefully through my body again. Here I was now, rushing uphill. I didn't look down because I didn't want to see the face of Petar Naumov, nor did I want to see his bloody hands lifting me up like the claws of a bird. Just a little bit further, another meter, just a half of an arm's reach and . . . there, my hand touched the warm green bunches of grass. I found myself on the plateau. The place was filled with joyful people walking around, alone or in groups, dressed in all sorts of different colors. Some musicians and a ladies' choir were there, as well as picnickers with innocent smiles on their faces. Everyone was in love with everyone else, seeing the best of each in the eyes of the other. They could see nothing bad, since nothing bad was there to see.

I waited for the sun to melt the frozen sweat off my face, for the wind to dry and bring color to my cheeks, then I let my hair down and put a scarf around my neck and chest, and thus adorned I was able to go and mix with the crowd. People were standing in large groups and I had to find my way through them. I was curious to know the reason for this gathering. In one place I came across the early lineup of the Yugoslav rock band *Bijelo Dugme* rehearsing a song, while an interesting exhibition of old jewelry drew my attention a hundred meters further. A group of girls, carefree and merry, interrupted me on my tour. I identified them as my high school friends. "You're here, Ema, great! We've been waiting for you!" "Why me?" I asked, instantly feeling embarrassed. My question sounded evasive, but I was just confused. "Forgive me, I am so glad to see you. What are you celebrating?" "The tenth anniversary of our high school graduation," they said, "but you won't celebrate with us, because you have things to do. Hurry up, they have been waiting for you to be able to begin the ceremony." "Who's waiting for me?" I asked nervously. "The choir. Hurry up."

So I did. I ran through hallways, peeked into every room. The rooms were messy, with pieces of clothing and shoes lying everywhere (these were dressing rooms, I supposed). Arriving miserably late at the scene of the ceremony, I stood at the doorway panting. I saw the women of the choir and started searching the rows in order to find the empty place intended for me. However, it wasn't empty—I was already *there*. I stared at myself superstitiously, as if I had just seen a ghost. All the singers were wearing long black tunics while only mine was red with a yellow sunflower embroidered on the chest. I stood out among them, resembling a secret amulet that protrudes from underneath a ceremonial suit. "Your dress is beautiful," I heard a comment from behind my back, coming from someone who was also observing me standing on the choral platform. "Isn't it strange that I exist in two places at the same time?" I asked without turning my head. I didn't care who my interlocutor was or what he looked like. What counted were the thought and the reasoning, and the fact that someone out there was capable of understanding that improbable occurrences are actually the most normal things in life. "The honesty of it is perhaps strange," my interlocutor replied, "but otherwise no, it's not. Bravo for the courage, woman!" But I didn't feel I deserved any credit for my supposed courage. I didn't want it in the first place, and it was no deliberate action. It was not real, I was dreaming, it must have all been a dream . . .

My nose was pressed into the pillow all covered in drool; wet and disheveled strands of hair were across my face. "Wake up, Ema! You're dreaming! Open your eyes now . . . There, don't go back to sleep, here I am . . . I'm right here beside you, are you awake . . . ? Yes? Good, excellent." The soothing words reached me from the space outside of my dream. They came from Žarko, the man with whom I shared my earthly worries and joys. He knew nothing of my dreams and nightmares. It's often the case that those with whom we share our bed and bread are unable to accompany us on the personal path that is charted within our own spirit. The path is different and uniquely painful for each person to travel, and cannot therefore be traveled all the way with any one person. There are people who live their entire lives without ever undertaking a spiritual journey, but there are those who do, and they know that the path must be taken; that there are dreams that must be dreamed and pains that must be suffered. They cannot escape them. Still, nobody should be alone in times of greatest suffering, when dreams become more difficult than life. There should be someone to wake you up at the right moment.

Chapter 5
Travelers Made of Glass Tread Thorny Roads

EMA SUCCEEDED IN getting where she was supposed to go, which meant that my mission was over. The most reasonable thing for me to do was to leave as soon as possible, right away even. Sticking around any longer was pointless, especially as I was already behind with my tasks and appointments at work. Still, I was having second thoughts; my determined and unwavering character, patiently developed over many years, wouldn't normally allow me to stay in a place uninvited—and character is destiny; mine and anyone else's—but a strange kind of curiosity, awoken by the mysterious ways of Emilija Savić, had gotten the better of me. The peculiar circumstance of helping Ema reach the plateau and the fact that I found myself there too, made me linger. Nestled in a rather small and thick bush, I was trying to figure out in peace what my next steps should be. Emilija Savić's last two dream adventures left me looking like I'd just escaped a war zone. I was bruised, covered in blood, and my clothes were torn. And yet, all of it would have been a minor inconvenience if it wasn't for the severe frostbite on my feet. Given that all this was happening in the month of June, even I, a man of formidable wit, superior intellect, and vivid imagination, couldn't find a reasonable explanation for such an unusual occurrence. "Petar, you're pretty well screwed here," I confessed to myself, right before realizing that I was just making excuses for staying a little longer.

Looking around, I noticed people in the distance, but there was nobody in the area around me; I was safe. Small branches of the underbrush were tickling my nose and forehead and, instinctively, I waved my hand to push them away. For a moment my eyes fell on tiny, perfectly round white berries of mistletoe. I knew that balm made from mistletoe cured frostbite. Well, wasn't that enough to make the heart of a man lost in a woman's dream rejoice and his soul sing? If it was *mistletoe* that I was placed next to amid all this, then I was clearly Fortune's favorite. I had to make a significant effort to remember the balm recipe from the herbal medicine handbook, but then I realized that it was useless to even think of starting the therapy without pork fat and plastic wrap. This threw me instantly into acute depression, during which I stared at my lifeless toes like a zombie. My only option was to go back to the apartment (thank God Anđa was out of town, attending a seminar; I wasn't sure how she would handle it if she realized I wasn't there). But how? Using what? I let out a desperate cry, dwelling on the possibility that Fortune was still around and that I was still her special pet. All of a sudden, I'd passed the terrace and realized I was back in my apartment—went to the kitchen and then to the pantry, made a quick stop in the bedroom where I took off the blue shirt and put on a white one. Here I was, preparing the balm, applying it on my deadened feet and wrapping them with plastic. Shortly after that I found myself lying in the grass on the plateau again, waiting for the balm to kick in.

Having been given such an unparalleled opportunity to do nothing, I decided to enjoy it the best I could. Seeking to avoid any kind of attachment to my surroundings, I was lying in the shadow of the underbrush without turning left or right, almost without any movement at all. I was thinking: if I don't notice other people, then they won't notice me—that would be fair enough. This was why I was considerably taken by surprise when I noticed somebody's shadow hovering over me. I didn't dare to raise my head. It turned out soon enough that there was no reason for me to anyway, since the shadow started moving down my stiff face, across my chest and stomach, and stopped at my feet. Finally, it took on a slightly bent human form and became completely still. A kind-looking man with short gray hair and a youthful face stared at me curiously and smiled.

"Sir, why are you here? Are you all right?" he asked while looking at the plastic wrap on my feet, which were, given our positions, placed very close to his face, practically right under his nose.

I moved back a little and folded my legs. I feared that my feet might smell. I remembered the funny odor of the pork fat while I was preparing it in the kitchen. Perhaps it had gone bad.

"I am fine. Thank you for asking. Excuse me, I won't stay long, I am just about to leave." The situation was somewhat unpleasant, and I was trying to get myself out of it.

"There is no need for you to hurry, this is a friendly place. Do you need some help? All you have to do is ask." His kindness was unrelenting.

"Everything is all right, believe me, apart from . . . apart from the fact that I am *incognito* here, and if you really want to do something for me, then I would like to ask you not to spread the word about my whereabouts," I said, swelling with pride for having the courage to speak the truth.

"Don't be modest, sir, it is impossible to be *incognito* here. The very fact that you *are* here means that this is the place where you should be. Therefore, welcome," my host persisted.

There was nothing to do, it seemed, but tell the whole story to this man, from beginning to end. Even if he failed to understand my position, at least I could expect sympathetic judgment on his part.

"Let me tell you why I feel like a foreigner here. You see, I arrived in this place as a kind of bodyguard. How should I put this . . . as some sort of packaging that goods in transit are

placed in. The packaging that says *Fragile: Handle with Care.*
I've come to realize that the path leading to this place is difficult,
paved with thorns, so to speak. Travelers made of glass often
tread it."

"Of glass, you say?"

"Yes, the ones that I'm talking about now are made of glass.
However, humans are also made of other materials that are
strongly represented as well. It depends, of course, on the type
of person."

"Hmmm . . . Go on!" I could tell by the look in his eyes that
he was interested.

"There are people made of rubber, plastic, clay, steel, slime,
foam, and so forth. The foam people can be compared, by the
essence of their being, to the glass ones. Their emotional frames
are similar in the sense that they have the same shared values,
but given the foam people's lack of any real substance, they are
dangerously exposed to all sorts of things; even the sun poses a
threat. The sun is their greatest peril, in fact. Both happiness and
sorrow melt them, make them perish. In other words, regardless
of the way they live their lives, their sensitivity is their worst
enemy."

"And what about the rubber ones?" the man was becoming more and more curious. Judging by the quizzical eyebrows
arched high beneath his hairline, I could see that his curiosity
wasn't feigned and that he'd succumbed to the charm of my
analytical exposition.

"They are indestructible. Since they are spineless, their flex-
ibility is shocking. They shamelessly stoop as low as possible
before everyone who can be useful to them and very naturally
seek to ingratiate themselves with those who can bring them
material gain. These are the ones who never go anywhere unless
somebody in a position of authority has already secured a free
passage for them, never condescending to wait in line for their
turn in life. Their filthy ways sully all that is good around them

but without affecting them at all—they are, in fact, completely unaware of the possibility of goodness in this world. They would be unworthy of mentioning if it weren't for the trouble they cause to the people in their immediate surroundings. Danger lurks within the amplitudinal range that their rubbery bodies. Spineless as they are, they cannot control the movements their bodies make. So, instead of returning to an upright position after stooping down, they start flailing uncontrollably at everything and everyone that fails to measure up to their perverted criteria. The extent to which they humiliate others is proportionate to the amount of time and energy they spend stooping down. In any case, as long as they are off balance, they are a hazard to others, as well as to themselves."

"And the slimy ones?"

"Ah, yes. They are comfortable wherever they are. They simply take on the form of whatever surface they are dropped on. Even if you stamp on them, they resist admirably. They don't break, they just spread and stretch until they finally free themselves from whatever is pushing down on them."

"What about the ones made of steel?"

"They deserve great respect. Steadfast and principled, they set high demands upon themselves as well as others. They don't break easily, but when they do, it's an explosion, and they never heal."

"Petar, will you be so kind as to place yourself within one of these categories?"

"I would say that I am one of those that are made of plastic. I'm light, mobile, difficult to break but easily dented. Not a day goes by that I don't get scratched or bumped, but all it takes is a little bit of warmth to smooth me and make things right. I am rather resistant to the slimy and the rubber people; those of foam always bring tears to my eyes, but when I see the glass ones I start feeling shivers down my spine. I literally shiver when I'm close to them."

"I presume it was a person made of glass that you helped?" The man guessed right.

"Yes, I did. Several times. Maybe she would have arrived safe and sound without me, without my help . . . Who knows? Maybe I should have been more patient, and waited . . . But I didn't. Whenever there was even a hint of danger, I jumped to her rescue."

"I also presume that you won't tell me who it is?"

Although the phrase *by hook or by crook* was nowhere to be found in the question that he asked, I couldn't help but feel as if wedges were being hammered underneath my fingernails in order to drag the information out of me. But my valiant heart endured this gruesome mental image and I adamantly declared: "No!"

"All right, Petar. I will leave you now, but don't take long . . . This is the first time we've had a visitor like you, and we don't have a set of rules for unexpected situations such as this one. I hope you understand that you have to leave. Goodbye . . . Since you've already found yourself here, I suppose it may happen that you come again—although, next time, with a reservation and a proper invitation. I wish you all the best," he said and left. I stayed, overcome with a strong feeling of serenity. How did he know my name? What kind of a place was this? I had to get out of here, but before that I had to remove the balm . . . I was better, my blood was circulating again. I raised myself and stood on my two feet, there . . . one more step . . . excellent. The outside world was calling me.

Chapter 6
Key Witness Takes a Vow of Silence

SITTING AT THE end of the long desk, in the remotest part of the teacher's lounge, Olga, the sociology teacher, asked: "Can this be true!?" The rhetorical cry traveled through the air for a microsecond before exploding over our heads. We all craned our necks, looking at her in silence. "People, Petar Naumov has gone missing!" she said without raising her eyes from the local newspaper spread open in front of her. "Missing? What do you mean missing?" The question came roaring in a perfectly harmonious polyphony. In a split second, the open space above the newspaper suddenly became densely dotted with teachers' heads.

I am pretty sure that I'd have gone over too—if only I'd been able to stand up. I felt as if some strange load had fallen on me and was holding me in the chair. I was aware that remaining reticent in such situations could be seen as suspicious. Indifference to spectacle is something that people always find irritating, and I was sure that the absence of any reaction on my part, accompanied by my perfectly peaceful countenance, wouldn't go unpunished. I knew very well that my outward composure was just a feeble cover-up under which a volcano bubbled, ready to erupt. Honestly, I was completely at a loss as to how I should behave. Finding an inconspicuous balance between my outward lack of interest and my inner turmoil was impossible at that point, and I gathered that, if I continued behaving so indifferently, I would soon be confronted with questions such as: *Ema, what is wrong*

with you? Do you know something about this? Why the secrecy?
Don't tell me it's something personal? A gloomy foreboding that I
wouldn't manage to escape such interrogation got me to my feet.

I stood up with such mental difficulty that I could almost
hear my body creak, like a rusty old machine being set in motion
again. The wildly excited bunch that was gathered around Olga
drooled over the possibility of a juicy scandal, especially since
it involved a morally impeccable man, generally considered to
be impervious to pacts with the devil. The newspaper article
gave rise to the spiciest conjectures based on facts as well as on
all sorts of insinuations, wild guesses, predictions, and doubts.
Petar was famous in town—a golden boy in the most positive
sense of the word, which made his actions all the more a target
for vicious barbs coming from the mental gutter.

I heard that he'd gone missing three days earlier and that
his wife Anđelija had reported his disappearance. The desperate woman was completely without a clue about her husband's
whereabouts, since she knew nobody had threatened or black-
mailed him. What's more, in the newspaper article, the missing person's wife had listed a number of reasons to justify her
belief that her husband couldn't have left home willingly. He
was a responsible man and a good husband—a bit of a hothead,
maybe, in his early days, but as levelheaded as it gets after set-
tling down with the family he loved so much. She dismissed
even the slightest possibility that he could have abandoned them.
Petar was a happy man, she claimed.

"Bravo Anđelija. I couldn't agree with you more." I heard my
thoughts coming to her support. "That's the way to defend your
dignity as well as your husband's. I pray that he comes back. My
heart is with you." And yet, at the same time, guilt swept over
me. My heart hid an unseemly, discomforting secret. Who could
I tell that he'd been with me for the past two nights, keeping
me company during my greatest ordeals, and that I'd got away
without knowing what had happened to him? How long had he

stayed in the cold, humid cave? Was he all right? Did he manage to get down from the snowy cliff? I wasn't ready to risk my reputation as a sane person, and I knew that nobody would consider dreams as valid evidence. They'd look for more, but there was nothing to be found—therefore, my lips were sealed. The fact that I was the only person who had seen Petar Naumov after he'd disappeared meant nothing. In this case, the key witness had consciously chosen to take a vow of silence.

* * *

The newspaper article had reported Anđelija Naumov's statement, and left it at that. The teacher's lounge, on the other hand, was swarming with mad ideas.

"That woman Anđelija is surprisingly naïve," said the math teacher, a well-known womanizer.

"What do you mean naïve? The woman knows her husband!" the librarian said in Anđelija's defense.

"And she loves him . . . she truly does," the English teacher said in a sentimental tone.

"There's certainly a lot to love . . . what a man!" the physics teacher raved.

"Okay, he *is* handsome, but a bit bland . . . His face is always clean-shaven and pale. Big hazel eyes, pearly teeth—he's kind of *wussy*, if you ask me. You don't have a real man without some manly sweat, beer breath, and strong, rough hands . . . that's what I say!" said the chubby coffee lady, excited and short of breath.

"Well, you can always ditch him if he gets any near you, at least that's easy!"

"Come on people, show some respect. This is a very unhappy situation!" said the moralizing school principal.

"An unhappy situation, my ass! I tell you—this is one happy love affair," said the school's legal adviser. Everyone turned their heads towards her and followed her confident exposé attentively. "I am personally acquainted with at least three young ladies from his office, all of them extremely attractive and pretty, who would jump into his bed at the slightest encouragement. Now, I'm not suggesting that your Mr. Perfect is a bad guy, I'm just saying that not many men would be able to resist the seductive charms of such ladies."

"Come on, make the long story short and share the rumor. If you know the ladies in person, then you must know if they actually had affairs with him."

"No, they haven't yet, which doesn't mean they won't—as soon as the one that he's with now becomes history. There's no doubt about it. As for Anđelija, apart from having illusions, she should really start having some doubts as well."

"Let's hear what our art teacher thinks about all this. Ema?" the school principal called me out.

"Nothing . . . I don't know," I said, lying.

After the bell rang most of my colleagues had classes to teach, so the jolly company thinned out. I was free, so I returned to the peace and quiet of my seat at the long table. My whole being stood in a spirited defense of a man I hardly knew. Was I defending him, or my own belief, which was based on a few images that I'd seen in my dreams? It was clear that I couldn't know what kind of man Petar Naumov was, but the feeling in my bones was telling me what he could or couldn't be capable of. I believed that he was faithful to his wife, which was something that had more to do with him than with Anđelija. I had no doubt that he had an eye for pretty women and that he wouldn't miss noticing a pair of long legs, a nice bottom, or big breasts. Maybe he wouldn't have a problem embracing an opportunity if it came along, but that wouldn't be more than a recreational pursuit of his carnal desires. He wouldn't see it as betrayal. The mental obstacle in his head, which lay at a completely different level, was based on his fear that a pretty face might hide something more, that luscious lips might utter words that speak to the heart, that a pair of eyes might have depth with some mystery to them—in a word, that some other woman could be the answer to all his questions. And that wouldn't be a betrayal (for all he knew, either there wasn't such a thing as betrayal or he didn't know what it was in the first place), but an irrevocable decision involving a new beginning that would draw a dividing line between him and Anđelija. That would be the moment when the crucial question would pop up: Petar, are you capable of hurting your wife that much? He knew the answer to that question. On the other hand, it's always difficult to know *where the shoe pinches*, so Petar didn't even try to find out. What if one actually fitted?

Petar was missing because he had been in my dreams, and it made me feel guilty, although I couldn't pinpoint why. I hadn't ever wished him to be there, at least not in a way a woman normally would. My conscience was clear before God; I examined my each and every thought. I paid special attention to the fleeting, seemingly inconsequential thoughts from the periphery of the mind, the ones that usually hide the real truth. As a *male*, Petar was not in them. I dared to imagine him in that way, picturing myself in a range of different roles—as a femme fatale, a betrayed woman, a monster, a saint, a witch riding a broom, and it wouldn't do. At the very hint of Petar as an erotic being, the image simply faded into thin air.

It occurred to me that, perhaps, I was unconsciously projecting onto Petar everything that I couldn't find in my man (or any other man I knew, for that matter). But no! I'd been searching for something that simply couldn't exist on this earth—two souls so tightly connected as to think or feel exactly the same thing. I couldn't find it. All my quests for truth came up against silent barriers. And yet, I had no problem spending the rest of my life going on my dream pilgrimages, as long as I went alone. What was happening now had to stop. There was no other way to banish Petar Naumov from my dreams but to stop dreaming about him. I was going to accomplish that by pressing the reset button on my life: no more retreating into my inner world. I was going to correct my fragile nature, arouse my dormant senses, and start living my life in the real world—as much as possible. I was guilty, but I was going to make things right. I just had to be determined in my decision. And I would be; I could do it.

First of all, I was going to figure out what to do about my general manner of perceiving the world. Was I supposed to reject it? Or just modify it? Maybe the key to a new outlook on life was to learn how to calmly observe this world where nobody really wants to hear what the other person has to say. People nod their heads all the time, but it doesn't mean they actually understand or approve; they simply do it to retain the attention of the person speaking for it's their turn to speak again. Winning the attention of people takes time, and the waiting is always difficult. The words fidget nervously at the tip of the tongue, waiting for the moment to come out in all their vain self-importance. *Me, me, me*—you can hear it everywhere, and all that should be communicated is lost. Even if they tried listening to each other, that wouldn't mean that one understood what the other was saying. And what if they *did* listen but then happened to misinterpret? Perhaps they would find offenses that weren't really there. Or they might place blind trust in the people they were talking to and let them get away with hypocrisy and flattery. But on the other hand—if people started seeing a possible duplicity in every spoken word, their skepticism would destroy the last traces of innocence in communication. The questions were endless, and I had to give up looking for answers that couldn't be found. I'd quell my rebellious being, and stop my soul from desiring what couldn't be—that one man would truly empathize with another.

I decided to dedicate myself to things that were ordinary and plain, things I would normally consider bizarre. I envied people who could take pleasure in simple joys. I couldn't, but everything could be learned, I thought, so I would try. I'd always been able to picture a life that would be easier and more relaxed, but since I hadn't succeeded in eradicating the chaos in my head, I defended my chaotic ways by seeing them as meaningful. Although my inner struggles had made life extremely difficult at times, I thought: If they were there, well, there must be a reason for them. I carried around the weight of the world, without knowing if I'd agreed to it, or if somebody had simply dropped it onto my shoulders. Nevertheless, I knew that my self-destructive turmoil couldn't be attributed to any external factors. I was the one with a dangerous weapon treacherously hidden somewhere deep inside. Everyone has it in them—this dark, venomous potion that kills you if you take it all at once, before the last drop trickles down your throat. This menacing substance is unrivalled in its deadliness, especially when compared to those hateful poisons that, very politely, give their victims just enough time for a quick autobiographical retrospective. Nature, however, a strategist without equal, releases the deadly poison very slowly into our systems, day by day, drop by drop, so that when death comes, even in very old age, it often looks like the victim has died of natural causes.

But then again—darkness has its opposing force too, which is light. Light defies the darkness of previous contemplation, and thus our salvation also lies hidden within all of us. I decided to focus on the outside world, and look for my salvation in all the beautiful things that meet the eye: clouds in the sky, flowers and butterflies, old gnarled branches and bird nests, white stones and sandcastles. I forbade myself to take even a peek at my darkness—if I gave it just a little bit of encouragement, it would overwhelm me again. So instead, I decided to banish my thoughts from the impossible world of my imagination and leave my solitary longings on the ash heap of personal history.

Chapter 7
The Importance of Hydro Potential in Maintaining Mental Hygiene

My wounds had healed and my feet were thawed, and if it wasn't for my churning stomach, one could say that I was physically ready to return to my ordinary, earthly existence.

My sense of decency, however, indicated a rather serious moral decline on my part. I knew that, if I wanted my life back the way it had been before my adventures in Emilija Savić's dreams, I still needed to make a great effort. At that point I started thinking how useful it would be to live in a city like Vienna, Budapest, Novi Sad, Belgrade . . . Those cities are all located on the banks of the mighty Danube, which was, in my estimation, among the few rivers that had the required water capacity to *wash away my sins* and justify the consequences of my seemingly irrational behavior before my boss, before my friends, but first and foremost—before Anđelija. My wife was away from home at an insurance seminar, and I thanked God for that. As much as I hated the idea of commercial insurance and despised salesmen's aggressiveness (which I could always sense beneath a forced smile and a polite veneer), I was ready to believe that the heavens intervened just so that I could think of a good alibi before Anđelija came back. If this whole thing ended well, God was my witness: the bitterest opponent of insurance would become a new policyholder! Well, so much for my integrity.

I was feeling powerless in my efforts to banish a sense of guilt that I couldn't quite define. Something cowardly had found its way into my heart, filling it with deep anxiety. Although determined to drive the fear away, I was blocked. Still, I had some common sense left; I could hear the words in my head: *Stay calm, Petar, and accept the situation as it is. Even if you wanted to explain yourself and your struggles, it wouldn't do, since they can't be explained rationally. Therefore, stop trying to be a hero—some spoken truths do make you famous and immortal, but others simply get you committed to a mental institution. I fear that the latter would be the case this time.* The soliloquy gave me some peace, allowing me to continue to calmly deliberate on water capacities and the suitability of rivers for clearing one's conscience.

The truth is that some people are born on the banks of the Danube, while others have the privilege of sitting at the edge of some other magnificent river; me—I had the West Morava. Now, it's not that the West Morava isn't good enough or anything like that; it's been put into folk songs and on painters' canvases; it's neither small nor shallow, and can be considered quite suitable for those guilty of, well, more venial sins. However, for a reprobate like myself, the West Morava was nothing more than a *brook*. I knew that I didn't have much chance there, since I was dealing with an honorable river that wouldn't go in for a business it couldn't handle. Still, I went. Squatting in the underbrush at the river bank, I started my negotiations inarticulately and insecurely. They turned out to be pointless. The West Morava seemed rather disinterested in me, and I could hear it gurgle: "If I were *the Great* Morava, I could perhaps try, but as it stands . . . no. Get away from my bank." The verdict wasn't uttered in a loud voice—the river went its way quite peacefully, so I reckoned that I could try and persuade it to at least try, since I had no other option. "No!" the river was categorical this time. "If you want to clear your conscience properly, find the place where I meet *the South* Morava, forming *the Great* Morava. Together, we may be able to help you. You'll have to catch the

train to Stalać that leaves at midnight. You'll be there by dawn."
Running against a rock, the river splashed these words into my
face and went on its way.

The evening found me sitting in a cramped compartment
of a train from Požega to Stalać. Packed into the compartment
with me were small-time smugglers dealing mostly in clothing. I
could tell by the lively communication and the familiarity with
which they addressed each other that they all traveled together
on the same routes at least twice a month. I overheard that
they were changing trains in Stalać, going to Niš, and from
there catching a train headed for Turkey. Since I was generally
lazy and prone to stick to one place, I found their undertakings
worthy of admiration, but I said nothing. I withdrew from the
conversation by closing my eyes and starting to breathe deeply
and noisily. I pulled this little acoustic trick to avoid getting
into any kind of discussion with them, knowing that any further conversation would likely involve tricky questions. I knew
nothing about trade, let alone about *fashion*; for me, clothes were
something that you use to cover your nudity and protect yourself
from cold. I didn't think they'd be satisfied with my appreciation
of their line of business, nor would they be interested in making
me one of their members—they'd surely think I didn't have
what it took—and that would be the moment they would start
interrogating me. Luckily, my trick worked; they believed that
I was asleep and kept their voices down, saving themselves from
the lunatic who was going to take a conscience-clearing dip in
the Great Morava in the dead of night.

I wished I could fool myself the way I fooled them. I tried
humming random tunes in order to fight back the restless
thoughts flashing through my mind. La-la-la-la . . . echoed in
my head. I managed to sort out my thoughts a little. Slowly, I
was able to deal with each one, one at a time. Firstly, I couldn't
believe how thoughtlessly and self-importantly I had ranted
about the *rubber* people to the kind man that I met on the

green plateau at the top of the snow cliff. I realized now that I'd made myself look like one of the rubber people's victims, and that my bitterness had been completely out of place. The problem with rage is that we always take it out on the wrong people, and this was one of those situations. I was comforted, though, by the fact that my violent outburst hadn't triggered any change in my host's attitude—his eyes had still shone with kindness and support.

While I was probing my conscience in an attempt to review my past behavior, the whole episode with the kind man that I met in that unlikely place suddenly got me thinking. What kind of a place was that? Who was he? The peace that he radiated was what intrigued me most. Such tranquility must have originated from some great suffering, I thought; like a hard-won trophy, it came to those who bore their cross with fortitude and patience. The man's sincerity was so clearly etched on my mind that it never occurred to me to doubt it; the peaceful expression covered his face the way a cassock covers the body of a former drug addict turned priest. Such people were true moral giants, and it looked like I'd had the honor of speaking to one of them.

For a while the image had me disconcerted. I was in the state people find themselves when they are honored with something they've wished for but haven't deserved. The next thought that occupied my mind was, logically, my strange entanglement with Emilija Savić. For the second, third, countless time, I was heading for her dreams. If those dream travels were a sign of something, I couldn't decipher it. Sitting in a stuffy compartment of a regional train with my eyes shut, I was going through the faces of (why be modest about it) the considerable number of women who had passed through my life. Their images flashed across my inner eyelids as I was trying to track down the face of this particular woman and see if it would lead me somewhere. I remembered that we'd been to several parties and weddings together, and that we'd exchanged a few sentences that provided

me with some biographical data from her life. She taught art in
a high school. She'd been living together with her boyfriend, a
lawyer, for years. She didn't have children. As for her age, she
was around thirty-five, thirty-six . . . maybe thirty-eight years
old—in any case, she was in her late thirties. That much I knew.
Even if I knew more biographical facts, they wouldn't be of great
importance—none of them brought me closer to her dreams.

The reasons for our dream encounters must have been rooted
deep down, beneath the surfaces of the ordinary. I thought it
was quite possible that Ema couldn't explain them either. If that
was the case, how was I supposed to know what was going on?
And it concerned me; it had become my business too. Now that
I thought of it, the strongest impression that I'd have during
those get-togethers was the peculiar attraction existing between
Ema and I, accompanied by a sense of incompleteness. I'd
always get the feeling that we were intending to say something
to each other, but we never did; I guess we were too cautious, too
frightened to become intimate in the presence of other people.
And so, we'd end up swallowing unspoken words like lumps
in our throats. I couldn't remember the topics, but they surely
weren't too deep or too subtle, with all the loud Balkan music
and the abandoned atmosphere that normally pervaded on such
occasions.

But now, when I thought of Ema's face, isolated from the
drunken crowd and carefully placed under my mind's scrutiny, I
could tell that, no matter how hard she tried to hide it, she didn't
belong there. I could see her face rather clearly: a sharp profile,
with prominent cheekbones and strong jawline; a smooth, pale
forehead enclosed in coal-black hair; small straight nose and
full, slightly stretched lips with just a touch of lipstick. She had
big brown eyes, wide open as if with surprise or amazement,
but often somehow dejected and sad. Nevertheless, it wasn't the
sadness that is reflected in the eyes of a melancholic or a defeated
person, but that of a person exhausted by her quest. She still had
passion in her eyes; she still had hope.

I wasn't much of a psychologist, but I could tell she was one of those people who had to try hard to be happy, while sadness came almost naturally to them. If I did manage to grasp at least some traits of her character (after having the nerve to go into such a detailed psychological analysis, it seemed to me that I did), it meant that I'd seen through the side of her that I could relate too. Any further identification stopped there. Unlike her, I was afraid of the dark passages in my mind and soul. I'd never allowed a personal defeat to cause any major setback in my life, and I believed that there was no emotional wound that a bit of worldly pleasure couldn't heal. There are thousands of distractions to divert unhappy humans and allow them to forget, to prevent apprehensive thoughts from finding their way in. We attend concerts and see films, undertake business activities or simply perform our daily routines . . . but still, sooner or later, existential restlessness creeps in. Although we try, every resistance, without exception, proves to be a Sisyphean task. Only some people are courageous enough to come face to face with their demons, and Ema was one of them. She'd joined the army of those who'd always go for the path less traveled if their hearts told them the path was the right one, although they knew that such paths are always traveled with *a spoke in the wheel.*

The arrival of my train in Stalać was accompanied by a squeaking sound of breaking (one would think that some spokes had been put in the train wheels too). The light gurgling of the Great Morava soon replaced the shrilly sounds of the train station, and I finally surrendered my irresponsible self, locked inside my sinful body, to the redeeming powers of the big river. I congratulated myself on the perseverance and moral strength that had got me where I presently was. Full of self-praise and boastful thoughts, I almost lost the track of what I was contemplating while still on the train. Although my present activities showed that I was completely determined to put myself through a rather peculiar process of physical and mental purification, my lack of focus on important things made me wonder if I wasn't merely a giddy-head, incapable of concentrating on spiritual things. Still, I wouldn't let myself be discouraged. After all, I did come all the way here in an attempt to find answers to the questions arising from Ema's dreams. I didn't see how I could help her resolve her inner struggles, but I knew that it was too late for me to quit. Where was she going? Was she on some kind of a quest? Was she afraid?

Chapter 8
Association Games Are for Experienced Players Only

BLOOD—LIFE.

Blood—death.

Blood—red, liquid, warm.

Blood—a bruise, a wound, a thorn.

Blood—a nose.

Blood—dense, thin, menstrual, virgin . . . irgin . . . rgin . . . gin . . . in . . . n . . . Anđelija could hear the word echoing, the last of many associations that flashed through her mind while she was holding her missing husband's blue shirt. She examined the shirt over and over again; she'd bury her face into the thin fabric, breathing in her husband's lingering smell, and then she'd suddenly press the blue fabric against her knees and start straightening it anxiously with her hands. She'd stretch and iron the blood-smeared cuff with her palms until five scattered bloodstains blurred in front of her eyes.

The red spots were all Anđelija Naumov could see. The image prevented her from realizing what the shirt, placed among the dirty laundry, was telling her. There were several things: that Petar had appeared in the apartment after his reported disappearance; that, in spite of the bloodstains on the cuff, he felt vigorous enough to undress and put on a clean shirt; that he had absolutely nothing to hide given the fact that he'd thrown off the shirt in such a careless manner, which further meant that his absence couldn't possibly have been ascribed to him sleeping around; and finally (but most importantly)—that he was alive. But no! Anđelija, anticipating the worst and thus already in a state of utmost misery, wasn't able to see things that way. She couldn't shake off the mental picture of her beloved Petar lying between the warm thighs of a girl's body touched for the first time. She was dwelling on the image until a sudden choked sob escaped her lips, interrupting her thinking and slightly obscuring the dreadful scene. The moment was right for Petar's imaginary shadow to appear and try to defend himself. Standing before his disheartened wife, the husband's image started parading in all the glory of his former faultlessness, offering proofs of unconditional loyalty and devotion.

This kind of guesswork was entirely foreign to Anđelija. She'd always stuck to raw facts, unambiguous manifestations, spoken words and clear gestures, and as far as her husband was concerned, she'd had nothing to object to whatsoever—it had been nothing but harmony and love. She'd rarely indulged in introspective ventures, let alone examining other people's thoughts. She knew that any such actions were like walking the devil's path—a good way to find out about things she didn't want to know in the first place. Only one-way tickets are sold for such a trip, considering all the risk involved.

At this point, Anđelija Naumov's nature was to thank for her escaping this maelstrom of associations by a hair's breadth. Her husband was alive, and that was the most important thing. She had no reason to doubt any justifications for his absence he might offer when he came back, which would surely be any minute now. She was about to go remove his pictures from bulletin boards, shop windows, and facades, and then go straight to the police and tell them to stop their search. She would have done it already if her practical self hadn't snapped her back into reality and warned her about the risk of such actions. It would be hard to explain that Petar was no longer missing while, *de facto*, he still was. How did she know that he was alive? On the basis of what? A blood-smeared shirt that appeared out of nowhere? The evidence was inconclusive and confusing, and she might also end up as the prime suspect. That was why she decided to stay quiet about her little discovery, and simply wait.

In the meantime, however, the lonely hours of staring at the telephone receiver and waiting for the doorbell to ring conspired against the rational side of Anđelija Naumov's character. They gnawed at the peace of mind she was trying so desperately to maintain. She was clutching at the last straws of her faith, and the tighter she clutched, the more they slipped from her hands. Doubt and anxiety were slowly taking over, arising from much deeper issues and therefore impossible to shake off as easily as the *blood* associations. She and Petar would celebrate twenty-five years of marriage in August. Their daughter Vanja, who was also twenty-five, had recently earned a college degree in special education and was, thank God, out of the country, working as a babysitter for a family living on the outskirts of Washington D.C., learning English and volunteering to gain some experience relevant to her career goals.

Anđelija was a woman of considerable ambition who never once loosened her grip on what she'd claimed for herself twenty-five years ago. But now, for the first time, she felt that her world was falling apart. She had met Petar at one of the birthday parties that were held in their college dorm. Withdrawn from the spotlight, she was observing him quietly from a corner of the room. He was with a tall, attractive brunette. What's happened to the beautiful blonde I've seen him with lately? Anđelija wondered. Love was finding its way into her inexperienced, virgin heart, and she, unknowingly, let it settle in. Was he a womanizer? Or were the affairs with all those beautiful women around him just steps he took while searching for his soul mate, someone who would make him feel complete? Now, that was the question that Anđelija didn't ask—as previously mentioned, she was far too practical for such deliberations and unwilling to occupy herself with riddles that couldn't be solved. So, although love struck and a little confused, she knew what she wanted. She was well aware that her looks weren't enough to attract Petar. She wasn't bad-looking, but she wasn't exactly from the cover of a magazine either. She was strong and well-built, with broad shoulders and big calves, and with rather prominent facial and body hair. Excessive hair was a problem for her, but, luckily, beauty parlors had already started employing depilation techniques that would do the trick. However, in complete contrast to her sturdy physique, her face had a loveliness to it—it was gentle, motherly, and kind. She combed her wavy chestnut hair neatly backwards to reveal her face and lend her the appearance of a 1950s screen diva.

She dared to want Petar Naumov, and she was about to get him. She wasn't *rotten*, though—being arrogant, obstinate, or rash was not in her nature. She would never resort to foul play just to get him, but she wouldn't rely on luck either. To get to Petar, she couldn't rely on the experiences of her former conquests, since there hadn't been any. Naïve, *self-taught* in a way, without a strategy or a plan, she started approaching him with what she had—her kindness, love, and loyalty. Firstly, she succeeded in getting close enough to him to be comfortable enough to knock on his door sometimes. "Could I stay in your room for a few hours?" she would ask. "There are four of us in our room. It's always crowded, I can't focus on my studying, so . . . if you don't mind." "No, of course I don't mind," he would reply obligingly. "I was just on my way out. Make yourself at home." And she would. When he'd come back, dinner would be ready and on the table—nothing festive, but tasty. The following day she'd wash and iron his shirt; each time she would indulge him in some way. And Petar swallowed the bait. He started skipping parties and coming back from evening get-togethers and dates to his apartment earlier than before, choosing to spend more and more time in the coziness of his room.

Anđelija tried to maintain an appearance of indifference at all costs. She knew that it was too early for her to open up her heart and lay bare the nudity of her soul before him. She hoped and prayed that she would recognize the moment when Petar was ready to make the *right* decision. It was a matter of life and death for her; but his *yes* was worth the risk. Patient in her abstinence and very careful not to pressure him in any way, she hungered for him without asking where he was going and when he was coming back; she rejoiced in his successes and comforted him when he was down. And his *yes* finally came. She was lucky enough to be persistent in the right way. She got exactly what she deserved—by choosing her, Petar didn't settle for second best; he gave in willingly and happily, and lived a life of bliss with her in all the years to follow. Maybe she couldn't give him what he truly wanted in his heart, but neither could all those other girls, so she felt at peace.

She'd given him plenty of love and attention—not many men could say they had the same. But then: click! Another unsettling thought came to her mind: what if she had been smothering him? She remembered her occasional outbursts of jealousy caused by anonymous phone calls. She could hear the flirty female voices again, asking to talk to Petar and then hanging up without saying who they were. Feeling threatened, she would have uncontrolled fits of rage. After they passed, for a long time she'd tremble silently in Petar's arms, allowing him to comfort her. He wouldn't defend himself; he had nothing to defend himself from, he'd say. She knew that he spoke the truth when he said that he couldn't be interested in women who were after him in such a vulgar manner, and that their marriage couldn't possibly be jeopardized by people like that; in fact, their marriage couldn't be jeopardized by anyone. But then, once again: click! Another vile association rushed to her head:

wasn't giggling and refusing to say your name in a telephone conversation something that teenage girls typically do? Could it be . . . could it be that Petar, her beloved husband, had gone crazy and become a *deflowerer*? The horrible images in her mind were too hard to bear this time. Well, if there was such a thing as a perfect moment to die, this was it, she thought in resignation, while some vague notions that seemed like part of some biblical sermon—*sowing* and *reaping*, *living* and *dying*, and the order by which they happen in life—rushed to her mind to give her comfort. She couldn't take it anymore. She'd spent too much strength winning Petar and keeping him by her side, and now she had nothing left—nothing to give her the strength to overcome the loss. All that was reasonable in her, all the composure that she'd struggled to assume, was now gone. She cried out in bitter pain, and, looking through tears, she had the impression that the bloodstains suddenly started to change color, take on different shapes and forms, expanding to swallow up the white surface of the shirt.

Chapter 9
Can Attempts at Self-Reformation Be Anything More than Glorious Exercises in Futility?

AFTER A LOT of dithering, whining, and hesitating, I made an important decision—the time had come for me to discipline my mind. My poor heart fluttered at the arrogance of such an undertaking. It seemed that I was *biting off more than I could chew*, but I could still hear the voice in my head that had made me set my mind to the whole endeavor in the first place: what are you so confused about? Isn't this what you wanted? Well, get to work then!

And so I did—there was no running away from it. I started doing abdominal breathing exercises next to the open window in the morning. My smoking habit made it a little difficult, but the effect on my circulatory system was good and I felt more relaxed. Then I decided to take rests in the afternoon; I wouldn't sleep, nor would I think—I'd just lie there, relaxed and tranquil. With my eyes closed, I could sense my restless thoughts buzzing and swarming somewhere in the back of my mind, but I was focusing on the mental picture of a kind of dark, flickering screen that I'd put up as a shield to prevent them from overpowering me. I was aware of the numerical strength of the army of thoughts that threatened to break down the fragile shield and invade the mind that *had turned against them*. Lying flat on the mattress of my bed, I was intensely conscious of every aspect of my present state: of my weight, of my every move and breath. My left foot lay underneath the ankle of my extended right leg; my left knee rested on top of the right knee; the heat of my left cheek met with the ice-cold palm of my right hand. I counted my breaths—they were noisy, slow and deep. I was making tremendous efforts of will, all in an attempt to weaken the finer sensibilities of my character; that way, I thought, I would eradicate once and for all the dream fictions that prayed on my mind.

And it seemed that two days of intense concentration produced results.

On the evening of the third day, which happened to be a Thursday, a housepainter came to our house to make a deal with Žarko about some work around the house that we'd planned for the weekend. After reaching an agreement, the housepainter left, and Žarko and I spent the evening watching an American comedy, *The Mexican*. Could there have been anything more logical than my having a dream in which Brad Pitt was painting our house in pastel colors? It was a healthy dream of a healthy woman, and since I was the woman who had it, Žarko and I automatically declared it a miracle. As soon as we woke up the next morning we opened a bottle of champagne; we raised our glasses to my unflinching resolve that survived despite the shaky foundations upon which it rested, and to the fact that my meditative sessions and concentration exercises had proven to be so formidably successful. The famous actor / sex symbol and I had spent the entire night in a very relaxed conversation. He complained about all the downsides of being a star, about the spinal arthritis that was causing him pain in his neck and shoulders (he even turned down his collar to show me where), about the burden of fame that was taking its toll on him although he couldn't quite pinpoint how, and he explained that he'd taken up house painting to help him keep his mind off things.

I spent the following day in a state of victorious euphoria, feeling immensely proud of myself, which was quite unusual for me. Since I'd always had a musical ear, I thought it appropriate to get up on an imaginary stage and belt out the National Anthem in honor of my firmness of character. As an incidental by-product of this pathetic scene (but a rather understandable one, if I may add), I even shed some tears. I imagined a press conference too, where I gave an exhaustive speech that slowly turned into a lecture on psychological self-help methods and their practical use for freeing oneself from emotional and mental chaos. Owing to my self-confidence, considerably boosted by my success, I'd grown quite eloquent on the subject—words followed one another in a perfect stream, and media reporters, listening to my speech in a sort of trance, barely managed to write everything down and release it. The news of my performance traveled fast, and the first reactions were broadcast that same night. They were numerous, both local and worldwide, but the most surprising one was the news about the unfortunate accident that had befallen Louise Hay.[2] They'd found her entirely green with envy and were barely able to pull her away from the TV set. She couldn't stand the fact that I had surpassed her and her self-help methods, nor could she admit that she was jealous. She was in such a bad state that they had to take her to the hospital. Misled by the greenish color of her face, the diagnostician wrongly put her in the isolation ward instead of the psychiatric one, which further postponed her recovery.

* * *

It turned out, however, that I, in fact, *jumped the gun*. I rejoiced in my success far too early. Nature proved to be a strong player and a formidable opponent—if nature can even be considered an opponent in the first place. As for my will—which was the product of my desire for some normality to prevail—it failed me; on Saturday morning, after a night of agonizing nightmares, I had a feeling that I'd hardly managed to stay alive. I couldn't tell

2. *Louise L. Hay*, a best-selling author of inspirational self-help books.

if I'd failed in correcting my nature or if I'd, in fact, indulged my true nature. Should perseverance be seen as the triumph of the firmness of character or as a weakness of spirit? And what about firmness of character—is it something that improves or impairs our nature? As for my nature, I couldn't be sure that it was made of a material that would resist the heaviest burdens, such as the awful, perverted dream that I'd just sprung out of, screaming.

I'd been standing in a bright, sunlit room, in the company of several young women. They were all pregnant, the size of each of their bellies depending on when their babies were due. If this was a waiting room of a gynecologist's office, I thought, then I must be here for the same reason. Without looking down, I stroked my belly . . . oh . . . yes. I was already far along. The thought of a baby inside instantly filled me with sheer bliss, over-powering me so strongly that I felt weak and had to sit down. All of a sudden, a woman approached me. She was a distant cousin of mine. Without any prior warning, she slipped her hand underneath my dress and put two fingers inside me. The pseudo-medical checkup was done in a minute. "Don't worry, it's not your time yet," she said and, responding to the call from the doctor's office, left the room. Ashamed and appalled, I didn't know how to react. The next moment I was already on the table in the doctor's office during an ultrasound checkup, looking at the monitor. It displayed a ghastly image; I was sure I wouldn't be able to survive it if it had happened while I was awake. My womb was a warm, slimy terrarium, where a coiled snake lay calm and immovable in a state of slumber. It was a python—yellow and glistening, as if made of sunlight. "It's all right, stay calm, you still have time . . ." I could hear the doctor's words. I started feeling some strange agitation in my stomach. "Time for what?!" I screamed in the doctor's face. "Cut me open . . . get this thing out! It's not all right, nothing is all right . . . ! I don't want to keep calm, I can't wait any longer for it to move, to wake up . . . It will tear me apart, I don't want to die that way!" No one was there to help me, and I suddenly felt someone pulling at my shoulder.

"Where's Petar?" I asked, all choked up. Reality was pushing its way underneath my tearful eyelids—I could hear Žarko's worried voice. "Wake up, Ema! Open your eyes. There's no Petar here, but there's me—that's as good as it gets." He squeezed his shoulder underneath my head, and I lay there awake, with my sniveling nose and glistening eyes, waiting for the sun to rise. "Who's Petar?" he asked. "An angel," I replied. "Are you kidding me? Ema, is there someone else?" "I'm not kidding you, and no, there's no one else. He can't be here, you can't be there—no one's threatened." "What do you mean 'there'?" asked the intrigued *earthling*. "What do you mean 'here'?" I replied from some kind of a vacuum-like void, with my feet of glass still not firmly planted on the ground of reality.

I was back to the beginning—alone in my own mental catacomb. I'd managed to fool myself, and for two days I believed that whoever sent Petar to be my faithful guardian could *take him off my case*. But the truth was—my case had been closed ever since I was a child, rocking in my cradle.

I was thirty-six years old. What had I done with my life in the years that had passed? What had those years done to me, apart from wrinkling the skin around my eyes and on my forehead? Deep inside, I was nothing more than a six-year-old, amazed at the world and anticipating a storm from a clear blue sky. But when the thunder started, I'd be crippled by fear and would retreat into my shell. For a century and a half, psychologists have been groping in the dark, unable to find an answer to the question: why can't reason control our emotions? As angry as I was with Freud and all of his successors, I quickly channeled my frustration onto—if you can imagine it—Nikola Tesla, our pride and glory, the most renowned Serbian scientist. I thought it preposterous that he'd had nothing better to do than to dabble in cloudy skies and proclaim that thunder and lightning were, in fact, products of electrical discharge. I'd have found it much more comforting if the entire business had to do with Thor walking among the clouds wielding his hammer . . . If I had grown out of my six-year-old ways, my maturity seemed to be reflected only in the fact that I could actually name and define some of my prenatal fears. I had made some progress, metaphorically speaking—if I'd been as tiny as a poppy seed rolling along in my tininess throughout my younger years, I was now nothing more than an ant. There was no danger of anyone stepping on me, though. I always made sure I was out of everyone's way.

Chapter 10
Both Dove and Snake Embodied in the Same Person—the Highest Level of Spiritual Maturity

Some people never realize that *silence is golden*; others do, at one point or another. I found myself among the lucky ones, but not before I'd wound up in a state of acute amnesia, unaware of the passage of time and the space surrounding me. The image that instantly sprang to mind was that of the brisk-walking young man that I would always meet in the same place every workday morning. He'd shoulder his way past me, leaving a trail of cologne behind. He'd probably have the earplugs of some state-of-the-art audio gadget stuck in his ears from the moment he left the house; unmindful of the cars parked along the sidewalk reducing the space for pedestrians, he would walk adroitly past and around them, neither reacting nor flinching when a passing car splashed muddy water from the road onto his pants. In general, the boy chose to be unaware of the world around him, and hardly anything could induce him to lose control, or *rhythm*, for that matter. I called him *the American*—I guess it was because his style and appearance were completely in line with the trends manufactured in the Western dream factory. I would mention him sometimes, here and there, as an example of a person who refused to grow up, deciding to see, hear, and feel only what he wanted to. Now, there was a difference between him and me—he chose that way of life, and in my case it just turned out that way. However, after all the experiences that I'd been going through, I couldn't help taking a somewhat different view of the whole thing. Now I understood and felt contrite for all the comments about him. Although my intentions weren't bad, I still felt like apologizing to *the American*.

I'd always been much more at ease when talking about myself than about others—what was wrong with me now? The poor *American* must have had awful hiccups,[3] given how much time I'd spent thinking about him while running my hands along the surface of the water of . . . well, I wasn't even sure which river it was anymore. Lying on my back, relaxed and lulled by the waves splashing lightly against my body, I was in a state of contemplation, meditating on the subject of *what am I doing in Emilija Savić's dream?* My thoughts took me too far; if it hadn't been for a big, loud wave that splashed all over me and threw me off my stroke, the chances were that I would have ended up somewhere in the Black Sea. Frightened, I managed to pull myself together after I saw a river barge passing by—so, I was still in the Danube. Was I in Serbia? I couldn't tell, nor did I dare to check. Soaked to the bone and without any identification, I knew that getting out on the river bank in order to start my journey back home was not an option. So, I started swimming upriver.

I stroked through the water forcefully. I was heading home, like salmon, whose keen sense of smell always takes them back home to spawn, though I can't say I was extremely *keen* on doing so. I knew that, unlike the fish, carnal activity was probably not the first thing that awaited me at home after going missing for quite some days. Still, I hurried onwards. I was swimming my way up the Serbian rivers, traveling fantastic distances, while the thoughts of Ema, now ominous and alarming, were racing through my brain again. Although I was on my conscience-clearing pilgrimage, I still saw everything: the loveliness of her face when she heard she was pregnant, the feeling of shame inflicted by the outrageous pseudo-medical checkup, Ema's womb with the majestic snake emperor inside: peaceful,

3. According to Serbian superstition, hiccups are caused by people talking about you.

powerful, beautiful, and—harmless, as long as it had food and felt wanted and nurtured. I saw the horror in her eyes, as if she'd just seen the door of hell opening before her . . . I saw it all, but I couldn't do anything to help her this time.

I was no longer in the mighty Danube; entering the waters of the Great Morava meant that I was making progress towards my final destination, but I knew that I had a long way to go . . . Although my strokes were still powerful and fast, the continuous effort of swimming upriver started to take its toll on me, and my strength and enthusiasm began to wane. The news that I had access to the contents of Ema's dreams even when I was absent didn't help, but I managed to *swim through* it somehow; however, the image of Ema waking up in the arms of her man while calling out my name almost made me drown. Disoriented and short of breath, for a while I resembled a tree trunk floating aimlessly on the surface, and it made me miss a turn at one of the confluences. I found myself at the edge of a county to the south of my hometown. My calves were swollen and I could feel stiffness in my arms; my worn-out muscles needed recharging. Yet I saw a silver lining to the situation—I could swim downriver this time, back to the missed turn, allowing me to gather my strength for the final section where I'd have to swim against the current in order to get home.

It turned out, however, that the physical weariness I was afraid of was no more than a hypochondriac whim. All the suffering that my body was subjected to—the hunger, the miles of river, the water temperature which was far from favorable—was gone the moment it dawned on me that I was, in fact, part of a rather exceptional story. I'd been secretly *claimed* by some woman's dreams. I felt enormous excitement surging through my body, sweeping away the fear and the fatigue. I came to see that, as much as I tried to unveil the secret of Ema's dreams, it was pointless; the more I tried to see in them, the more intangible they would become. This revelation infused me with great energy, and suddenly it didn't matter that my whole life was turned upside down—I felt good. I stroked confidently through the waves, not letting them impede my progress. Just one managed to catch me off guard and submerge me under the water. Some of it got into my mouth and made me choke slightly, and it felt like some of Hesse's poem "Wilted Leaf," which I'd read a long time ago, had gotten stuck in my throat:

Play your game and don't resist,
Take it calmly, without sound.
Give yourself to the wind to break you
And take you home.

Yes! Home was *within* me. I carried it by my two feet, like snails that without conceit or shame bravely go through life with their homes on their backs, unafraid to expose them to the world. My house was my name; my dwelling was where my identity lay, and yet I knew so little about it. I barely suspected where it was; I guessed—somewhere close to the heart. I had groped to find it, stumbled and fell, but now I knew it existed, and I couldn't stop looking for it and wondering about it.

If nothing that was happening to me rested on reason, was it worth employing these newly-born thoughts, clumsy and raw, in an effort to provide an explanation? Wouldn't it be cruel to let these spiritual fledglings into the arena in which even my well-formed thoughts had a hard time making sense of things? That's why I decided not to touch them; I'd keep them warm and water them, with salty water from my eyes if that was what they needed, so that they'd grow and mature, and become worthy of being spoken. I had to be patient for that to happen; I'd *resist the resistance* of my set ways and surrender myself to my fears, so that they could slice and grind the stale contents of my mind and make something brand new out of it.

For Christ's sake, Ema! It suddenly became clear. How did

you miss it? How could you let the old fear of snakes take you in? Wisdom is what you were so afraid of, and you shouldn't have been. There is a place within you made for it. Your innocence resembles that of a dove, but, make no mistake about it—the true counterpart of the dove can only be the snake . . . If you can read my mind the way I can read yours, listen to me: when the snake visits your dreams next time (if there is a next time)— embrace it, and do so in peace.

I still had no sense of time; on the other hand, I had a rather exact notion of my whereabouts. I entered my building and started climbing the three stories of stairs, feeling the water from my wet clothes drip down my back. Somewhere up high, maybe in the attic, I heard the door, and then quick shuffling of someone's feet—some of the neighbors had a visitor. Some woman probably. I wasn't looking forward to the imminent encounter; I didn't expect it in the first place, since it had seemed that the building, with all its tenants, was sound asleep. There was nothing I could do, obviously—I couldn't get away. I hoped it was somebody I didn't know. I straightened my back, put my chest out—since wet clothes are said to be so erotic, I thought that it was a good way to alleviate the lady's shock and to end up with the least possible embarrassment. Luckily, the scenario didn't come to pass: the sound of the footsteps had suddenly gone silent, and I heard another door open and close, only this time the sound appeared closer and clearer. I was relieved—it must have been one of those neighborly visits, which, again, always implied human relations that were rarely simple, but still intimate in their own peculiar way.

Three more steps, two, one, and here I was—at my door. Against all logic, although I was completely wet, I wasn't shivering with cold or shaking for any other reason. Staring at the door-plate that had the names of the two Naumovs inscribed in brass letters, I was trying to trace the joyful *home sweet home* cry somewhere inside of me . . . but to no avail. Then I thought, maybe I should look for a feeling contradictory to joy—dread, anxiety, or any other form of uneasiness, since our thoughts and feelings often trick us; we expect to be joyful about something only to find ourselves in a state of misery the very next minute. Still nothing. I seemed to be in a certain kind of emotional limbo, experiencing *a calm before the storm* that I would doubtlessly confront very soon. I grabbed the door handle—it was locked. I knocked twice, but there was nothing except dead silence behind the closed door. I knocked again—finally, I could hear the shuffle of Anđa's feet. "Who . . . is it?" I heard her stammer. "EHYEH ASHER EHYEH," I revealed myself to my wife while entering the dimly lit foyer. She welcomed me as if I were nothing less than the Jewish God—with incredulous joy and amazement. As if suddenly feeling weak, she pressed herself against me. The tight squeeze soaked her clothes with the surplus water that was still on my body; she gave me a hug that most probably saved me from freezing to the bone and catching some awful fever. Better than any mistletoe balm, Anđa did the right thing—and healed me. I wouldn't have expected anything else.

"You're back already?" I murmured with my face buried in her hair.

"Already? Petar, I came back ten days ago."

She caught me off guard. I hadn't prepared my defense; I had neither alibi nor courage to defend myself, because I didn't know what the truth was. I could only say what I felt and suspected to be the truth. My body slumped onto a hard wooden chair, and I asked for some *rakia*.

"Will it sound stupid if I tell you that I went out to get some coffee?"

"Very stupid!" I could hear her voice resonating near one of the upper cabinets in the kitchen, accompanied by the clinking of spirit glasses.

"Will you trust me if I tell you that I wish only the best for you?"

"Not more than that?" She was not to be mollified.

"And that I love you?" I sweetened up my assurances.

"Petar, are you all right?"

"I'm fine. Don't ask me anything else."

"What is that supposed to mean?"

"I'd have to tell you everything."

"You think I couldn't take it?" She knocked back her drink, trying to forestall the impending shock.

"Everybody carries their own burden, and this one is mine. I carry it easily; it'd be too heavy for you, and you'd suffer needlessly."

"Is it another woman?" The impatient, irrepressible question flew my way.

"My darling, I'm all yours—from the waist down and all the way *up to my neck!*" I stood up from the chair and took her in my arms. I didn't waste time; it wouldn't take her long to realize that *the head* was left out from my cry of devotion and loyalty. Pressed against each other, with our chests heaving and panting, we both felt the assertions of loyalty materialize in my groin area.

Chapter 11
Better to Believe and Not to See than to See and Not to Understand

THE AUDIO TAPE that Žarko pushed into the cassette player in his car produced a short, sharp click! announcing that it had settled comfortably in its place and picked up where it left off that morning. *Ostani noćas i sedi . . . kad si tu*[4] . . . While he was adjusting the rearview mirror, Žarko caught a glimpse of his face—still boyish, without a single gray hair in his fair, somewhat long, ruffled hair. Although he had a few wrinkles here and there visible on the clean-shaven skin, he still looked young. His eyes were grave and intent, and his piercing, hard look made his face appear more serious. . . . *Nekom će suze, nekom biser i . . . rođeni . . . ve-ruj-mi.* The last words burst into syllables, completely detaching him from the gruesome routine of a lawyer's work. Hard faces of his clients—angry, irascible old men fiercely battling over petty portions of land followed him like shadows on his way from the office to the parking lot. He could hear them pleading, cursing, swearing on their mother's grave, insulting and spitting in each other's faces, and then seeking justice from him. Desperate, dumbfounded mothers trailed in their wake, demanding their sons be released from prison immediately, because . . . they'd been framed, set up! They would never throw a broken bottle into a friend's face! Was it possible that their sweet boys could have done it? It seemed like only yesterday

4. Pop song "Bato" performed by the Yugoslav band Kaliopi (1987).

they'd been just babies, suckling their mothers' milk and falling sound asleep like angels on their swollen bosoms.

He knew that he'd escaped them only after he slammed the car door and turned on the music; he relished the intermezzo, feeling as if he had taken a strong antidepressant. A ten-minute ride and there he was—in the southern part of the city, at the doorstep of his and Ema's *warm family nest*. This wasn't some tacky metaphor; it was objective reality. Ema and Žarko's apartment often looked like a nest in the literal sense of the word—with little branches and leaves, specks of food and dust, clothes scattered around and glasses from two nights before. In their case, cleaning up wasn't a matter of order and discipline, but of sudden enthusiasm and pleasure that would come out of nowhere. When that happened, everything would be spick-and-span; the apartment would glisten as if a real-estate agent were about to visit. If only those were the moments when unexpected guests would drop by! But it was always the other way around—the messier the apartment would get, the more cluttered it would become, giving rise to all sorts of gossip about the lack of proper and timely cleaning in their household.

The moment Žarko entered the foyer he knew the day was one of the *mad* ones. Judging by the vacuum cleaner that lay disassembled and abandoned on the floor, he guessed that Ema's plans for the day had been somewhat different in the morning. They had fallen through; Ema was sitting at the table that she'd offhandedly wiped clear with her arms. She had pushed aside all the little boxes, bags, packets, and other knickknacks in order to make room for herself and the books that were now lying on the table, and was bent over them, looking from one book to the other. There she was, he thought, pitting the wits of philosophers and poets, distant from each other in space and time, against each other again. He approached and, kissing her on the head, saw who they were: Søren Kierkegaard and Petar II Petrović Njegoš. Slowly, on his tiptoes, he circumvented the aura of peacefulness in which she'd enveloped herself and, like a reptile, moved silently and adroitly to the fridge.

If there had been pleasures that he missed out on in his life with Ema, one thing was for sure: he'd never been threatened by starvation. The situation with cooking was pretty much the same as with cleaning. She wouldn't cook every day; she'd wait to get into the mood for spending hours at the stove. Luckily, sooner or later she'd go on a mad cooking spree, and they would end up with substantial food reserves stockpiled in little pots, jars, bottles, and bowls. Even if she had never cooked, they would have found some solution to the problem of providing meals for themselves. Eating well was important for Žarko, but it was far from being the most important reason for choosing Ema as his life companion. Now, he knew very well that any other Balkan husband who considered himself a man of dignity would spit on this kind of life—every other man would have already walked away. Living with a woman who refused to have children, with whom months would pass without having sex, who didn't iron her man's pants regularly, and who couldn't recognize the smell of shoe polish if her life depended on it—this would be considered an intolerable idiocy and an utter disgrace for a respectable patriarchal man. Fortunately, he didn't feel the need to explain himself to anyone, since he couldn't expect others to understand what he himself often failed to understand. He knew it couldn't have been any other way—nor should it have.

"Well, weren't Aristotle and Jakob Brucker the poor idle things!?" Ema's cry came from the room. "Why *poor?*" Žarko replied with some difficulty, his mouth full of succulent meat-stuffed chard rolls and yogurt. "What I would like to know is where did the bread they ate come from, since they deemed earning *bread by the sweat of one's brow* to preclude one's engaging in philosophical thought!" she said in a louder voice this time, getting closer to the kitchen. She stood in the kitchen doorway, trying to recover from her repulsion. "Unbelievable!"

she said indignantly. "It's hard to accept that the people who are thought to be some of the greatest minds in human history denied the possibility that those who earn bread by the sweat of their brow might have the tiniest shred of intelligence," she continued in a manner that was getting more and more vehement. "I understand that material comfort and physical idleness don't necessarily imply the absence of psychological torment. But, goodness knows, if psychological torment is added to the exertion of the body and the pains one goes through to make a living, that torment can actually be beneficial."

She corroborated her claim by listing the names of the thinkers that she thought would support either the first or the second line of thought, and he had to agree. When it came to topics such as this one, he wouldn't dare challenge her authority, given how little he knew about the subject. Nevertheless, he knew that whenever Ema started throwing fits, letting her angst and self-imposed riddles overtake her, nightmares would follow. He wished he could share some of her burden, but he couldn't—the weight of the world she felt on her shoulders had little effect on him. He was aware of how little he understood, and since he wasn't even sure he knew how to keep his own head above water, he never allowed himself to question and judge her ways and interests. What they *could* do—which was exactly what they did—was to hear each other out and save each other by being so different. He wouldn't let Ema lose herself in the tormenting labyrinths of her mind, and she wouldn't let him get lost in the mundanity of life. That was their symbiosis.

The evening started well. Intrigued by the vehemence of her afternoon soliloquy, he became interested in expanding his own knowledge of the subject and began asking questions. They both knew that his condescending questions and her explanations were nothing more than a game that they both pretended to fall for. The erotic being of Emilija Savić lived deep underneath the surface—suppressed and sublimated, pushed almost into oblivion, but still not eradicated. Sexual abstinence was not a matter of some firm resolution that she had made; indeed, given the choice, she would gladly choose a body for which sexual arousal was not such an issue. But she couldn't choose. Overshadowed by some other, much heavier obsessions, her sensuality had gone into a strategic retreat, saving its strength and trying to survive.

Ema's desires hadn't disappeared; they'd withdrawn to a place that was deep and far away, and yet they weren't unreachable. Her sexuality could be awoken, but it was a matter of Žarko's patience and skill. He knew that, and he'd realized that the frequency of their sexual intercourse depended solely on him. He couldn't expect her to seduce him, to cuddle and caress him; she'd never feel such an urge—her blood was too cold for that. Ema's carnal lust dwelled deep in the subliminal, underneath the crust of her consciousness. She did, however, constantly yearn for physical contact: for a hug, a soft touch, a fleeting kiss, all kinds of everyday proofs of affection. But lust! Making her lust was a challenge. The TV set would have to be turned off. A stimulating conversation would have to flow—an ardent discussion celebrating beauty and goodness in the world. Vangelis's instrumental "The Conquest of Paradise" would have to play quietly and for countless times in the background, and finally—Ema would be sitting on his lap. Grateful for having someone who understood her *madness*, she'd kiss him passionately, hot-blooded and aroused, letting her suppressed urges slowly overtake her. The wanton Ema would dare the saint cheekily, and the saint would let her do it. And both of them would enjoy it, like every time was the best ever, swearing that they'd do it all over again the next day.

And yet, the next day would never happen. Despite being unable to understand her obsessions and fears, Žarko felt a strange sort of responsibility for Ema. He cherished her like a precious thing locked inside a box he'd never thought of opening. He preferred to admire her blindly. He could take a peek inside the mysterious box, of course; but what if he couldn't understand what was there?

Chapter 12
Quivering Creatures or Bug-Eyed Monsters?

MY DREAM FROM the other night began so peacefully and ended in complete terror. Raindrops—sunrays; cloudy skies—clear blue skies; serenity—horror; what were they? A part of *the ever-whirling wheel of change*? Plagued by this question, I spent the entire next day bumping into people and things. The day went by, the night came, and I still couldn't disentangle myself from the state of bewilderment that the previous night's nightmare had left me in.

For the first time, one of my harrowing plunges into the subliminal went by without Petar's support. He would have helped me, I had no doubts about that—if he'd been there, he would have known how to *fix* things. Was it too pretentious of me to believe that his absence this time was all my doing? Maybe the man simply had an innate sense of spiritual adventurism, which had led him into my dreams only for a short while, to entertain himself a little and then simply go his way. Whatever the case, I missed him.

I was afraid. Although reluctantly, I couldn't stop thinking about the gift I experienced in my dream but felt I didn't deserve: motherhood. In my dream, my animal instinct had finally prevailed against what I'd considered in reality to be my better judgment—I was expecting a child. I'd often imagined being a mother, and the thought weighed heavily on me. Being aware of all the misery and unhappiness that earthly existence entailed, how could I bring myself to give life and take responsibility for my children? They would end up ravaged by their urges and desires. Even if some greater misfortune didn't befall them, just the thought of them suffering from unrequited love, getting caught up in whatever web of schemes and intrigues, and struggling to clear the obstacles on their life's path . . . It was more than I could accept! I didn't have the courage to take that kind of responsibility. I'd felt there was something arrogant about bringing children into this world—like consciously bringing *lambs to slaughter*, without any guarantee that I could save them. Knowing one's limits is always a good thing, but there's always the question: why can't I do more?

I always hid from the world, and while hiding from the bad things, I also missed the good things. Most bug-eyed monsters crawling around Planet Earth are nothing but specters, seen through the magnifying eyes of human fears. Fear makes the quivering creatures—and I was a good example of this—rather calculated in their ways. The quivering creatures go through life precariously, on glass feet, knowing very well that every careless step can become a matter of life and death. That's why, for them, taking delight in things always implies anticipation of a potential mental and emotional breakdown. I, for one, hadn't experienced any great misfortunes in life; there hadn't been any extreme inconveniences either. And yet—the fear was there. Where did it come from? Could the knowledge that bad, awful things existed somewhere out there make the fear so strong? Obviously, yes. Whenever my mind dwelled on such thoughts, I would remember Kundera's words: "Having a child is to show an absolute accord with mankind. If I have a child, it's as though I'm saying: I was born and have tasted life and declare it so good that it merits being duplicated." So I wasn't alone in my private, experiential philosophy, which was soothing; there were others who sealed their destiny by deciding to renounce the immortality achieved by producing new generations of humans.

I couldn't take my hand off my flat belly, nor could I stop picturing an imaginary scene with Kierkegaard and Njegoš sitting opposite each other. I'd worked painstakingly to set up this little gathering, and I wasn't going to let a nightmare ruin it for me. Finally, there they were—two men who might have searched each other out, but were unaware of each other's existence, and their paths had never crossed. Although time, as measured by the calendar, had been on their side, the space between them had proven to be an insurmountable obstacle. The year 1813 was a glorious one: the two wonderful minds were born—one in Denmark, the other in Montenegro—without, however, any real chance to meet and communicate. Nevertheless, their meeting was meant to happen, and I was overjoyed now, because . . . their encounter seemed just *so* right.

They took delight in their conversation, picking up on each other's words, exchanging energies, their palms and faces sweating in excitement. I was observing them from the nearest place where I could do so discretely and unnoticed. I knew, though, that if I were to smash a glass on the floor, the noise would not even make them wince—for people like them, tranquility was a result of concentration and obsession rather than merely of silence. My initial intention was for them to have their discussion while walking, but I dismissed the idea, partly on Kierkegaard's behalf. Despite the immense proportions of his mind and spirit, I thought that the short and hunchbacked Kierkegaard might not feel quite at ease before the impressive physical qualities of his Montenegrin peer. Although endowed with considerable imaginative potential, my earthly eye couldn't help seeing them in their human form, as creatures of flesh and blood.

And here they were, sitting at a primitive wooden table, their elbows propped on the outer planks. Two beautiful heads, one facing the other. Njegoš's face was pale and manly, framed with tidy dark hair. His eyes were also dark, with a look that was grave and deep. Kierkegaard—a boy with curls that fell over the frame of his glasses, with the clearest blue eyes behind them. His face was clean-shaven and anemic. It didn't take long for them to pass the phase of introduction; the initial veneer of politeness began to crack, and the fire took over. Their burning spirits cast away the layers of their imagined corporeality, one by one, until their souls were laid bare, yearning for interaction. Both of them were in their thirties—Njegoš just before writing *The Ray of the Microcosm*, and Kierkegaard while preparing *Either/Or* for the publisher. I could hear the Dane's broken yet charming voice: "All my suffering is rooted in the imbalance existing between the corporeal and the spiritual. Is that my cross, my limitation?"

"It's all part of our earthly existence," replied Njegoš steadily, with the assurance of a man who had already deeply deliberated on the subject, picking up on Kierkegaard's thought as if it were the most natural thing—as if they were weaving an intricate tapestry of thoughts in perfect harmony. "One has to be cunning to feel comfortable in this dog-eat-dog world. Our will is fickle and greedy; it breeds awful desires. After pleasure comes boredom . . . then pleasure again, and then boredom again . . . until we reach a state of utter despair."

"I hide my melancholy and my sorrow from everyone. I take it hard that others don't understand me . . . They don't even understand how sorry I feel for them for not understanding me. However, I know that if a man is blessed in the religious sense, his earthly living is nothing but torture, and I've come to accept that," whispered Kierkegaard, convinced and reconciled.

"Nothing else can be done but to accept it," Njegoš assented.

I let the philosophers converse and then go on with their lives the way history testifies. Their souls struck up a rapport that I, who introduced them, always knew they would. I pined for unknown and distant souls that would be *mine*—the ones with whom I would have the same affinity. Was I never to meet them? Wasn't there some kind of eternal magnetism of thought that drew two souls together if they recognized themselves, even if centuries or worlds stood between them? Was Petar Naumov's presence in my dreams one of the ways in which spiritual forces softly but persistently invade the harsh, crusted reality?

* * *

It was midnight. I crawled into the bed and pressed my body against Žarko's back. His warm body pulsated with the healthy energy of a man who, in his waking state, could feel joy, sadness, anger, and peace. My thoughts, heavy and deep, made it less easy for such feelings to rule my being. My palms and feet were cold. I impatiently pushed them under Žarko's warm armpits and his heavy, crossed legs. Not even in his sleep did he refuse my *cold* self. As if carefully opening up to me he turned a little, adjusting his body for me to snuggle at his side and fall asleep peacefully.

I felt my body descending into the state of slumber; my eyelids were closing, and I could barely keep my eye on the beam of streetlight shooting through the window. Before escaping to the other side of consciousness, I thought I heard the pages of the books flapping lightly in the next room. They were still turning, testifying that the conversation between *the great ones* had not yet ceased. Good night, they said; good night, I replied, thankful that the questions that I was now posing had already been answered a century and a half ago.

Chapter 13
The Mirror Is a Lie—Eyes Are Turned Inwards

WHEN ANĐA SAW me, she became overwhelmed by intense emotions and gripped my wet body so hard that she became soaked; and now, reinstated as the most desirable woman in the world, she really made me sweat. There was no doubt that such a turn of events had a beneficial effect on me; in other words, if this hadn't happened, it would have meant the end of me. However, I didn't manage to escape the fever that came on afterwards. My temperature soared and I was in a hallucinatory state for several days and nights. Faces flashed before my watery eyes; some of them I saw clearly, others were just a blur. Anđa's face was one of them, but there were also other people that I didn't know. The face that haunted me the most, persistently and at regular intervals, blinding me like a searchlight in a high-security prison, was the pale face of Emilija Savić.

The expressions on her face varied; at times they appeared enraptured, at other times thoughtful and melancholic, and very rarely flushed with anger or quiet defiance. Once she appeared in a company of men engaged in a lively conversation. I deduced from the way they were dressed that they must be historical figures—*gone stale*, so to speak. Fever-stricken as I was, their exchanges, discontinuous and irregular, seemed just a loud sustained noise. Somehow it became clear, though, that the gentlemen were Njegoš, the Montenegrin bishop and poet, and the Danish philosopher Kierkegaard.

I welcomed that first morning when I had more or less recovered. My head was clear and I could stand firmly on my own two feet. There was only one surviving remnant from my feverish nightmares: the face of the woman who was definitely reshaping my destiny. And she was doing it with my blessing. I *stashed away* her image in a safe place in my mind, leaving it for further analysis and contemplation that I would conduct later.

For the moment, I just wanted to go outside. Anđa didn't answer when I called her name—was she at work? At the market? At the pharmacy? I didn't know, and it didn't matter. All in all, her absence meant that I had recovered—otherwise she wouldn't have left me. Before leaving the house, I looked at myself in the mirror and was startled by my frail appearance, weakened during the illness. I did my best to make myself look decent, and stepped into the outside world.

I felt light in every sense of the word—fatigued by the temperature, mentally ravaged by nightmares, generally drained and weightless—but still, I felt fine. After the morning rush, the streets and the sidewalks were almost empty. From one of the cafés I could hear the melody of an old, tender French song . . . just a few more notes and I would remember . . . yes! That was it . . . "Tombe la neige." It seemed like life was being played to the rhythm of dance music. I reveled in one of those beautiful emotional states that humans, always ungrateful and never tired of pleasure, wished could last forever—states that never would. My case was no different—I saw my face on a piece of paper attached to a power pole. I winced; the sight froze me on the spot. *Missing . . . Please call this number . . .* Suddenly everything became clear. There was another *me* on the bulletin board across the street, missing one eye. Then another *me*, with a beard, on a lamppost. I liked myself with a beard. I kept my eyes on it long enough to realize that I was grinning like a fool, almost narcissistically, at the idea of growing a beard. Petar? Hello!? I could hear a little voice in my head trying to snap me out of it. I started thinking hard, and since I was fresh and rested, it didn't take me long to figure out why my face was everywhere:

Anda had reported my disappearance.
She didn't report that I'd come back.

And she wasn't going to—she thought I was crazy. Insanity is a disease that makes a normal person feel ashamed, which in no way meant that my normal wife didn't love me. It meant that she wasn't going to take me anywhere with her until I got better; or, to put it more precisely, until I started behaving the way she thought a healthy person should.

Although all that had happened lately couldn't be explained rationally and I wasn't able to say what the truth was, I felt that my feet were firmly on the path towards discovering my own personal truth. I wouldn't let the strangeness of it all put me off my quest. Not for once did I consider backing off—but I didn't really have any choice. I didn't care if everybody thought that I'd gone off the rails and was just crazy—I knew that the Petar who awaited me at the end of that path was a new, *whole* me.

From now on, I would be rational when it came to other people, but not when it came to myself. I'd never been a gambler in my life, always kept my composure, always been Mr. Perfect. I'd consumed an optimal dose of ethics and religion, hoping to get by. Now, I was stuck between two realms—one was the earth, the other was the sky. The sky is an ambiguous concept, though; sometimes it descends so low that even the lowest of earthly creatures find themselves with their heads in the clouds. Some people, like me, end up there without being asked, but there's no point in trying to fight the inevitable course of events. I'd given in to something I didn't know the cause of, aware that the consequences to my life would be profound. I'd smashed

the crusted nothingness with my head. Having survived my
fears and ignorance, I eventually saw things in a different light,
which would never have happened if I'd remained, stubborn
and self-complacent, in the humdrum reality of my everyday
existence.

I felt myself *growing*, as if the invisible ties that had bound
me were snapping under the pressure of the power of the secret
revelation inside of me. Suddenly, I realized: the reflection in the
mirror is a lie. Our eyes are, in fact, turned inwards, but nature
has done everything to obscure the simple fact that our true
selves lie inside of us. One should take a good look inside, *pick
at one's soul* in order to see who one really is and what one should
do to realize one's true potential. But is that really possible,
caught in the snares of middle-class reality? Is it possible at the
desk or at the kitchen table, in the marital bed, on a construction site? Is it possible, surrounded by people expecting things
of you, depending on you, ordering or conditioning you? Is it an
honorable thing to fulfill the obligations that you have towards
yourself, and neglect those you might have towards others? Yes!
Both honorable and necessary.

The first thing I did was take down the pictures of me from
the places where I could do it without drawing attention to
myself. I entrusted the rest of the work to a dark-skinned guy
working for the City Parks Department. He refused to, at first,
but yielded after I gave him some money. Staring at him per-
suasively, I convinced him that he was doing the right thing.
I assured him his soul would stay intact and his conscience
clear—except, obviously, for the part where he accepted the
bribe, thus giving in to corruption.

Since I had no special plans for my morning promenade,
I decided to let my feet take me wherever they wanted, and
here I was—after numerous crossings and intersections,
bends and curves—right at the entrance of the office where I
worked. Standing in front of *the hand that fed me* and which

I'd unhappily *bit*, I knew very well that nothing I could offer as explanation would be acceptable to anyone in their right mind. Nevertheless, given that I'd just found myself there, without any prior preparation or rehearsal, I went inside without actually feeling any of the anxiety or confusion that would normally be expected of someone who had gone AWOL and was about to explain himself to his superiors.

There was a meeting in progress in the *commander-in-chief*'s office. My appearance there caused the scene to freeze; resembling well-practiced players of the *freeze tag* game, everyone present in the room was left motionless and holding their breath. The cigarette fixed between the index finger and the middle finger of the hand of one of my female colleagues stood frozen halfway to the ashtray. One of my male colleagues had been interrupted just as he was about to politely put his hand over his mouth to mask his yawning; now he was staring at me with his jaw wide open and his arm raised like a Nazi salute. The coffee lady became inadvertently bonded to a cup via the frozen stream of coffee pouring out of the pot. My lovely associate was in the middle of trying to adjust her stockings without anyone noticing, by pulling one of them up above her knee. What would normally have been a pleasurable but fleeting sight lasted for quite a few moments. My eyes rested on her beautiful, slender thigh for a while and then moved all the way up to the red nail dug into her flesh. From there, my eyes shifted quickly to the paralyzed face of the office director—my boss. "Here I am, people!" I said with a clap of my hands.

My words snapped everyone out of their strange stillness, and judging from the absence of any kind of bewilderment on their part, I concluded that, apart from having been in shock, they also must have suffered from acute amnesia—they saw nothing unusual in me being there. "So, Petar, we have a deal!" my boss said. Having no idea what he was talking about, I prayed that he'd go on so that I could figure out what he meant. And he did.

"We have no major projects until the fall, so what you're going to do these next two Thursdays is go to high schools and talk to the seniors who intend to study architecture. We all know that our profession has fallen on hard times, so you'll try to talk them out of it; as for the ones who have definitely made up their minds—arrange a private session or two on behalf of our organization. You can set the time and date when it suits you," the boss said. I nodded in agreement. "Okay people, enjoy your holidays! See you in September," the boss finished and, with his hand in the air, led the staff marching out of the office.

My feet definitely knew where to take me now. With one worry less, I surrendered completely to their will and ended up at the town library, where I requested books by Njegoš and Kierkegaard, as well as Maslow—an inner voice was telling me that I would need *therapy* after I was done with the first two. Some of the books weren't allowed to be taken out of the library, but they knew me there as a responsible person and an avid reader, so they gave me permission to take the books home with me even though it was contrary to library policy. For the second time that day, I'd circumvented the rules. Oh well . . . what else could I do?

* * *

It's a good thing I'd never studied philosophy (although I almost had), so I didn't feel I needed to read everyone and everything even if I didn't want to. But as a secret aficionado and dabbler in philosophy, I could choose and devote myself to only what I felt like reading. I couldn't have gotten into Schopenhauer and Hegel, for example; those two couldn't coexist with Fromm and Maslow—they simply weren't *my thing*. Now I was going to delve into the work of the Dane—he can't have appeared in my dreams for no reason. Such a decent man wouldn't have knocked at my door unless he really had to.

When it comes to my personal choice of philosophy books, it had happened only once that I *got my fingers burned*; it was with the young, ingenious Otto Weininger. Some strange restlessness had made me plunge into the work of the twenty-year-old wunderkind. I don't remember the details, since the immediate shock had erased the sentences that I'd read from my mind. The only thing I remember was that I'd dropped the book and stood there shaking my hands, as if I still couldn't believe that I'd managed to free myself from the sticky web of some deadly spider.

Regardless of whether the images in my head came from my own nightmares or from Emilija Savić's dreams, they aroused my curiosity. No wonder that I spent the entire following night browsing the yellowed pages of the old books that I'd borrowed from the library. Some of them brimmed with hard sentences, expressing decided finalities and maxims intended for *all eternity*; others were full of melancholy and wistfulness. They created an atmosphere of hysteria: the spirit aimed for lofty heights but then came crashing to the ground, and the higher up it went, the harder it fell. In everything I read that touched me I recognized a part of me that had been hidden in the dark, waiting for some stimulus that was intriguing enough to elicit a response. I knew that this reading experience was going to reveal a lot about the woman in whose dreams I'd arrived uninvited. There were passages that didn't resonate with me. I found many sentences strange and unclear, but the ones that I *got* filled me with a wondrous excitement.

Feeling as if made of air, weightless but somehow huge, I soared upwards and made a hole in the sky with my forehead. Dense and moist clouds lightly swayed under my feet; there was nothing but endless azure around and above me. I wasn't sure how long I'd been enjoying this bliss, when my body suddenly remembered *home*, and started longing for it. The battle between the body and the spirit resembled hand-to-hand combat. Reality was there, omnipresent and stark; it hadn't moved from my side for a second. I knew that my earthly days were still to be lived, and that adventures such as this one were something that I had to accept as occasional heaven-sent adventures. I'd lost my orientation and it took me a while to figure out how to leave the blissful state as painlessly as possible. I took a deep breath, moved the clouds with my hands and looked down. And it was a sight to see.

Chapter 14
Crinoline Made of Light

It LOOKED LIKE it was nighttime, and yet it wasn't. A murky and damp afternoon, with drizzling rain and grayness that pressed down heavily upon the road that I was following, found me barely able to see where I was going. My feet, faithful servants, walked the path unquestioningly, with a steady rhythm, without any fear or doubt that the path might lead me astray. The darkness was becoming denser and denser, and by the cold gusts of wind that I felt in my nostrils I could sense that there was a storm coming. I froze in place and listened carefully; I could hear a dull, hollow sound in the distance, ominously announcing the storm's approach.

There was no balance of natural forces here—the disaster that was coming my way had all the power, while I was powerless. If I decided to wait, it would be the last thing I'd ever waited for. I had to go back immediately, so I *took to my heels* (my *Achilles' heel* was located a little higher than that, in the area close to the heart, so running posed no problem; my feet were healthy and strong). I ran as fast as my feet could carry me. The truth was that I had no idea where my starting point had been or where I was heading; therefore, I didn't know where I was going *back* to. It seemed that someone knew it *for me*, otherwise one would assume that I was just rambling around, which I most certainly wasn't.

I advanced with the confidence of a headless fly and arrived relatively quickly—arrived where? I had no idea. The haze cleared up in a rather peculiar way. It didn't disappear or become less dense or compact; it simply retreated and, as if it had been sliced through, it was still surrounding me but only beyond a radius of two steps. I was standing in a spotlight, all alone on a stage. I raised my eyes, trying to see where the unusual light came from. I noticed a square patch of blue sky that looked as if someone had *uncorked* a piece in the darkness and made a tiny hole so that bright azure could find its way through. I lowered my eyes and stepped forth—the light followed. I made a step back—the light went with me. I found the game interesting; as if wearing a crinoline hoop skirt made of light, I was enveloped in a beam that followed each step that I took and kept the damp grayness away. The dull surroundings outside the beam persisted, however, waiting for the light to go out so that darkness, sustained by the power of human fear, could impose its rule again. I was clutching at this moment of bliss as if *at a straw*; I felt so light that I knew the straw would hold. Confident, even cocky, with my arms spread wide and my head tilted back, I was spinning around to the rhythm of the "Blue Danube" waltz, feeling euphoric . . . I was the chosen one . . . the chosen one.

The state that I was in couldn't last forever—that much I knew. Still, I allowed myself to be happy. All of a sudden, the circle of light started narrowing, withdrawing before the darkness. The beam was fading, and soon my eyes would be confronted with complete darkness. But before the light went out completely, I saw a pair of feet placing themselves right before mine.

Hidden in the darkness and feeling no surprise or astonishment, my visitor and I stood there face-to-face—without touching or making a sound. My hands, with my fingers intertwined, rested in the lower part of my back. I didn't move them; since the situation didn't require resistance or physical intimacy, there was no need for it. I felt someone's warm breath on my neck. The being standing next to me was of flesh and blood. I raised my head slowly, and my nose grazed against the fabric covering his chest; I could smell the traces of cologne. And then our lips joined—simply, without searching or hesitating, with the passion of those who had looked for each other endlessly and were finally together. Something mad was happening in our heads—as if our brains had turned to liquid and were flowing together, becoming one in a way that denied the possibility of them ever separating again. The rest of our bodies were paralyzed, showing no sexual interest whatsoever. My nose was in his mouth, in his eyes; he swallowed my cheeks, drank my tears and saliva, and all was warm and intimate, plunged into bottomless desire. And then, in a wordless presentiment of a good-bye, the kiss acquired the strength of the kisses given at airports, which are always the final ones, despite the lovers' promises. Was it really a kiss? It epitomized the fierce struggle of those who wouldn't settle just for *pain* in this life.

Suddenly, like when a washing machine breaks down during a spin cycle, our thoughts began to separate from the walls of the tub that the perfect union of our two heads created. They fell in a pile and were slowly cooling off. We picked them up randomly, it didn't matter—his or mine, they were all the same. At the same moment we realized that we weren't really waiting to board any plane—after such a union, a good-bye was impossible. Having been joined both by our lips and our minds, basking in serenity, we pressed our foreheads together and listened to the blood pulsing in each other's heads.

I woke up the next morning without screaming, without tears on the pillow. The dawn was breaking outside; Žarko's cell phone alarm would go off soon. My *wandering* head needed to be adjusted to my slumbering body. While putting my head back into place, I touched my face and my hot, swollen lips with my fingers, and then sniffed them, hunting for the smells from the past encounter. It was so fresh in my mind, and yet it was already a memory.

Finally, I saw things clearly: spiritual quests were not in vain. Existence wasn't meaningless for those who searched. There was perfect love and there were souls yearning to be joined in true intimacy, at least in some other dimensions. Carnal desires had nothing to with it. Nor did sex. I was given an opportunity to experience pure bliss, and I knew it was now and never again. One doesn't get a second chance to experience such things, nor can we expect to find pure bliss anywhere in the waking state of our earthly existence. Reality, in which only suffering is pure and happiness never is, ruins everything. I didn't feel any guilt; I sinned against no one—welcome back to my dreams, Mr. Petar Naumov.

Chapter 15
The Proud Owner of Two Worlds

When I thought of myself stretched among the clouds, the image that sprang to mind was that of a gymnast performing on the rings in the final heat in which all is to be decided. He does his very best, focusing all his strength into the arms that, stretched into a calm and unwavering horizontal line, keep the rest of his body perfectly vertical. I was doing the same, more or less, pushing the clouds apart in order to make room for a beam of light to swoop down, so that the one who danced below me could take a few more steps before the darkness fell on her again. I was doing my best, which, given my present physical weakness, wasn't much. Eventually my muscles went limp, my hands weren't strong enough to hold the pressure anymore, and I fell through the clouds. Only two and a half somersaults on my journey down and I switched from headfirst into the upright position, finding myself face to face with Emilija Savić.

"Why are you looking at me like that, Petar?" Anđa asked me in a choked, subdued voice. She had been sitting at the foot of the bed for God knows how long, waiting for me to open my eyes.

"My dear Anđa, the apple of my eye"—I uttered a rather stupid metaphor, which, perhaps, wasn't completely arbitrary. The tender look in her eyes, *sweetened up* to the extreme, had to be the clear reflection of what emanated from my eyes. My look must have been extraordinary, fierce, and teary. Both geometrically and factually, I was looking at my wife, but, as usually happens with faulty projections (and this one was one of them), I was looking at her because I had no choice. But Anđa was worthy of being looked at that way. Was it important who or what really made the eyes swell with tears and emotion?

The extraordinary union formed between Emilija Savić and me in her most recent dream hadn't been driven by carnal impulses. My body was simply *there*, disinterested and paralyzed, as if this thing with Emilija Savić was *none of its business*. My head was under attack from countless sensations, and the fact that I still had it on my shoulders seemed like a miracle. Strong impressions, still fresh from the dream, gushed out of my eyes and overwhelmed my wife, who, like all the lucky ones in this world, found herself in the right place at the right time. Confused and confounded, she didn't know what to do—should she indulge in the unexpected tenderness? Or should she run away? If there was anyone in the world that I knew well, it was my wife—she would recover in a split-second. Here she was, already on her feet, straightening the sheet on the bed quickly and energetically:

"You're not well, Petar, you're pale . . . let me bring you some soup."

"I am fine, I'm just a little tired . . . but soup . . . yes, please . . . thank you, and don't bring it in here, I'll be in the kitchen in ten minutes."

Thank you, I could hear her repeat my words while going towards the kitchen. Shaking her head in silent disbelief, she couldn't be more bewildered than she was now. I could see that she found my behavior suspicious, or at least strange. How was I going to tell her that, as far as I was concerned, we were *in the same boat*? Tormented by the same questions, each of us was there with our own silences and our presentiments of what the future may hold in store. My imagined sins and adulteries ravaged her heart, and she refused to believe them, screaming NO!

in the face of the possibility that she'd been betrayed, whereas I nurtured and cherished a secret, a newly discovered meaning of my life.

Finally, I came to understand fully that a tremendous invisible force ruled the corporeal realm. If I said that sadness is the reason we shed our tears, that the steps we take are driven by our will, that our changes in facial expression are induced by love, hope, anxiety, desire, anger, resignation, exhilaration, despair—one could say that I was *reinventing the wheel*. Still, to me it was a revelation to finally understand that all worldly, palpable things were nothing but manifestations of our inner forces. Also, I came to realize how deeply submerged I was in the realm in which the body didn't care about the head, and the head functioned separately from the body. Everything had its place—the soul belonged to the heavens, and the body to the earth.

I knew that the fact that I was looking for proofs in my worldly, personal experience was a sign of my weak will. I had observed religious practices, but without conviction or faith. In the end, it turned out that, at the age of forty-seven, I needed a crazy dream encounter to feel what it was like to surrender to something without calculations, inhibitions, or delay. I came to comprehend the feeling of loving someone as much as I loved myself. Eternal in its duration and endless in its scope, this love also possessed the quality of making you powerful enough to let the beloved one go, if that was how it had to be. In a word, the force called *Agape* had swept me like a tornado, in a magnificent cyclone.

The previous paragraph betrays the chronological order of events in this story. It hadn't been easy to understand what had really happened to me in Emilija Savić's dream. When I first came to my senses I was utterly confounded and, to be completely honest, scared to death. I remembered our enraptured spirits, the unprecedented interaction that abolished the physical

boundaries existing between the two of us. Two souls became
one. But I didn't feel my body—as if it wasn't there; as if all the
blood had rushed out and ice had been injected into my veins.
What could possibly have happened to make my body remain
unresponsive where no real healthy man's would?

Now, even in my waking state, I still couldn't be quite sure
that my body was actually functioning. I touched my neck,
made a few circular movements with my head . . . everything
seemed to be fine. Then I checked my legs. I bent my knees,
stretched my toes, tried to get up—and succeeded. I reached
the window in three steps. So everything was all right. I didn't
understand. Could *black magic* be at work here? Heaven knows
that jealous women go to any length to keep their man by their
side. I shook my head in disbelief. Don't be ridiculous, Petar,
I told myself. Do you really think that Anđa would be capable
of doing something like that? I was sure I wouldn't have fallen
under any spell that easily, knowing how strong my spirit was.
There was no way she would have lied to me and resorted to
voodoo. In our house we had a special love of the cult of so-called
white lies—light and harmless, they were a perfect way to spare
the ones you loved from pain and unhappiness. Hard truths
would be given in small, digestible doses, so that they would
lie easier in our hearts. On the other hand, at the very hint of
something more serious we had a hawthorn stake and a wreath
of garlic stashed in a safe place.

So much for my being slow and incapable of acting *like a real
man* in the proximity of a lovely woman during a dream encounter. Nevertheless, since certain things in life impose themselves
on us so sharply, as if begging to be understood, I could only
agree that understanding *late* was better than *never*. Only after
a while did it dawn on me: a dream with Emilija Savić in it
could never be sexual. Be that as it may, I was richer for this
otherworldly, reviving adventure. Just knowing that such a world
existed was a tremendous energy boost, making every burden

of daily existence seem bearable. A by-product of this new situation—collateral damage, even—was my need to be silent. Not many thoughts were worth uttering anymore, it seemed, nor were many topics worthy of discussion. Everything that was crucial yesterday was simply strange now. If I wanted to become a spokesman for truth, I would have to come to terms with the status of *madman*. It meant hurting people—Anda, first of all. I couldn't do that. I'd already hurt her enough. I was a happy man—I wasn't a hypocrite or a liar, I didn't *fish in troubled waters*. I hadn't intruded on anybody's territory in my conquest of this new world; I'd been taken by Ema's dreams—I was *conquered by them*, but by no means imprisoned. I was allowed a semblance of freedom, in the sense that I seemed to be in control of all aspects of my life and able to make choices like a normal, mature man, although I knew I was on a kind of rationally inexplicable mission that was part of a larger, mysterious plan.

A warning flashed through my mind that I should get a hold of myself—I'd studied the situation and made an extraordinary discovery, and now I should let the things cool off a little. I took the advice of my wiser half readily and let my eyes roam around the room, resting on the pieces of furniture and scattered trifles. I didn't feel particularly interested in any specific object in the room, but I was happy to know that I was able to keep my focus. My jacket, casually thrown on a chair, drew my attention, and I started observing it more closely. Creases and folds gave the coat an interesting form that could be quite a challenge for . . . let's say, a sculptor. All of a sudden my jacket became *alive*, trembling slightly on the chair. I was on the verge of believing that I'd also acquired telekinetic powers when the familiar melody accompanied by a vibration made me realize that my mobile phone alarm had gone off.

I used the mobile phone only when I had to, and although I looked upon all those *smart* gadgets with complete disdain, I had to admit that they came in quite handy to distracted types like me, who couldn't keep track of everything they had in their hectic business schedules. I took the phone out of the pocket and read: *Thursday June 25 at 11, high school seniors.* "Anđa!" I shouted. "Is today Thursday?" "Yes," she answered. "Good," I said, already making a perfect clothing combination in my head—light-blue shirt, fashionably faded jeans, sandals, but where was my daily planner? And what was I going to talk to them about . . . ? Jesus, I didn't even have a presentation or anything, and they were going to look to me as if I were God himself. A fake one, obviously. Still, they didn't know that. *She* worked in that school, but the summer break had already started, so the chances that we would meet weren't really that big . . . I guessed.

"Petar, the soup will be completely cold by now," I heard Anđa's voice from the kitchen. I sat down, had my soup, and got back on my feet again. All I needed was my cigarettes, my pen, and my planner, and I was ready to go. The moment my left hand grabbed the door handle, I realized that one of Maslow's books that I'd taken from the library the other day had curiously found itself underneath one of my armpits. The book had flown from the shelf above the TV set, reaching speeds comparable to that of a thrown knife that strikes right beside the terrified face of a circus maestro's target. This time, there was no doubt: telekinesis was at work. Someone's spirit was demonstrating its power; was it Maslow's? Or Emilija Savić's? Maybe mine? I stepped outside, with the book firmly pressed underneath my armpit.

Chapter 16
Parallel Track as Excellent Hideout

"Do you belong to *Kachalov*?"[5] I asked a small black dog that had been following me ever since I'd left the house. All curly-coated and dirty, the creature kept pushing its muzzle against my heel. *Jim, give me your paw for luck* . . . Stopping briefly and bending down, I recited Yesenin's line into its pricked-up ears and instantly felt the healing powers of poetry in everyday situations. The poem unwound in my mind to the last line . . . *Lick her hand tenderly for me, for everything I was and wasn't guilty of* . . . producing heavy tears that hung in the corners of my eyes. Rays of morning sun hit the dog's gray, moist muzzle and the creature, as if bewildered by my strange behavior, tilted its head to one side and looked at me with an expression of blank curiosity.

I'd need luck today. I'd be addressing around thirty high school seniors who had chosen to enroll in art academies, and they'd be very keen on hearing what their art teacher had to say. What should I tell them without making it a cliché? What if I *lost it* and my speech turned into an embittered tirade by an unaccomplished woman in her late thirties? I could picture myself talking gibberish and, awkward and nervous, failing to present my arguments with the conviction required to sustain the illusions of youth. The worst thing was that I, as an art historian, couldn't address them from the standpoint of an artist.

5. A reference to the Russian poet Sergei Yesenin's poem "To Kachalov's Dog."

However, I'd never considered it to be a small thing, given that the number of art consumers was in constant decline. I feared that there would come a time when poets would write for other poets, composers would make classical music for classical musicians, opera singers would sing only before their colleagues. Ironically, those whom the arts could benefit the most, by helping them to escape from their humdrum existence, were the least interested. Their limited, one-track minds, flying disdainfully on the wings of their own ignorance, would dismiss the mere thought of engaging in any creative experience.

Be that as it may, I wasn't going to let myself shatter their dreams or fire them with false enthusiasm. I was going to ask them if they'd taken into consideration certain things that I thought were crucial in the matter: for instance, whether their choice had to do with their natural affinities—in other words, whether their enthusiasm was actually based on some kind of proof of their talent, or whether it was a matter of some unreal fascination with one of the arts. And fascinations are often dangerous and deluding for the young and the inexperienced—they already see themselves on stage, in a gallery, at a literary soiree, swept up by the applause while being presented with a prestigious award. Not to mention having a street with their name on it! Or a square, maybe, in the center of which their monument would stand—for all eternity.

I'd talk to them about the importance of recognizing one's own vocation, which is the only true path to self-actualization. I'd tell them that they should persevere in everything they do, not allowing ill-intentioned people (and there would be quite a few of those) to make them quit or start hating what they'd initially been passionate about. Every success implied hard work, but only in the arts did it have a higher cause. And if one day they realized that there was no difference between *I wish*, *I want to*, and *I have to*; that they rested while working and worked while resting; that they were getting paid for their work although, in fact, they'd be ready to *pay* to do whatever they did for living—then that would be a true triumph. Few were those who answered to no one but themselves, who obeyed unreservedly only the voice in their heads telling them what to say, write, paint, or sculpt. If there was a dry place in this *vale of tears*, that was it.

This was, more or less, the main idea of the oratorical performance I had planned. How it actually turned out, I couldn't quite say. Between the first meeting I held with my students after classes and the moment in which I was now, there stood an impenetrable wall bearing a huge, glaring graffito saying: *I barely escaped (or not?) bumping into Petar Naumov.* We were approaching each other from opposite ends of the school corridor. Every inch of my body fell into a state of utter unease. A few more inevitable steps and I would find myself face to face with him. I instantly grew weak and felt as if all the strength that I had went into my toes and left me completely numb and with an impression that even if I wanted to stop—I couldn't. This encounter had to be avoided. I couldn't start a conversation with something as mundane as: *Good day, how are you . . . I'm very well, thank you . . . What brings you to our school . . . ? blah blah blah.* I simply couldn't. Revealing the truth—what truth? whose truth?—was out of the question. God, please help me! I thought. I wasn't ready to confront him—not here, not in this bare life, in this harsh reality. Our corporeal selves wouldn't remain silent; in all our previous encounters they had been placed on the margin of events—now they would want *a piece of the action*, and would ruin everything. Please, God—he and I had met where only the spiritual dwells, in its purest form. Would all that now be lost? And God heard my prayers: Petar went into Room 32, and I, relieved, held myself against one of the radiators in the corridor next to the open window, trying to catch my breath.

The evening came, and heavy thoughts triggered by the morning's events wouldn't leave me in peace. I tried to find

distraction watching TV, but in vain. I flicked aimlessly from
one channel to another, alternating between the only two channels that I thought could provide me with content I would find
interesting. If I didn't love Žarko as much as I did and if I didn't
respect his taste and his choices, I'd have the other twenty-eight
channels deleted, choosing to voluntarily expose myself to this
media shortage. I was hoping to find something that would keep
me distracted for the period of time necessary for all the complex, long-simmering questions inside of me to cool off, allowing
things to regain their proper perspective. Thousands of *whys*
gnawed at me like unstoppable hordes of hungry mice trying to
get a bite of a dry and stale piece of cheese. Ah, if I could just
find an easy way out and respond with the ignorant, defiant *who
cares!* I had tried this a couple of times, but it didn't work. My
search for answers tortured me. It was like toiling endlessly on
barren land. Only occasionally did my efforts bear fruit, and I
would be provided with a meaningful answer.

Why do you go through life with a heavy heart?

The land is hard, parched and cracked, and it easily breaks
the thin skin of tender human feet. No matter how hard we try
to keep our emotions deep down, they rise to the surface. No
matter how hard we train ourselves to hear only sweet melodies,
cries and moans are still loudest. Nevertheless, I still raise my
head (often sharply, giving an impression of conceit on my part),
because I love to see the sky grazed by the treetops and the warm
light shining on me with kindness like a Good Samaritan. I
expose my face to feel the wind that caressed so many on its
way to me—among them someone who is my kind, someone
I'll never meet. Whenever I feel that I've regained my strength, I
know that my weak, earthly form has been infused with a draft
of God's mercy, and I am able to go on.

What's this weight of the world that you carry on your shoulders?

People who walk this earth are nothing but artificial forms
with masks on their faces. The physical shape of humans covers

the essence of their being. In its falseness, the shape gets distorted, because the essence, silenced and repressed, doesn't give in that easily—it pushes and shoves, insists on its truth and importance, pumping blood into the cheeks and making the face contort in silent screams. Only the most refined hypocrites master the skill of controlling their reactions; however, if one is observant, their eyes, ice-cold despite a soft smile, speak volumes. Out of a thousand people, 980 are fakes. There are so few people who don't feel the need to *talk rubbish*: someone's gained or lost weight . . . oh, her new hairdo looks great on her . . . those new glasses don't do her justice, really . . . this guy's earned a fortune; alas, this guy is ruined.

I've noticed: I've put on some weight. I have a slightly sagging double chin. I can't fit into the skirt I bought last year. But my non-material *I*, although continually accorded a status of pathetic, second-rate subtenant of my material form, feels fresh even when my body isn't, and screams in disapproval at being equated with the picture in the mirror.

So, what are your options?

I've discovered parallel tracks. They are walked by groups of people who are soul mates among themselves. We pick up on each other's words—if there's a thought bouncing around my brain, they'll know what it is. We're connected by our thoughts and dreams, and happy to know that the other one will come whenever he's needed, in whichever form—we'll know. The sky, the treetops, and the people walking my track with me have made me love life.

Chapter 17
That Life-Changing Quiver That Makes All the Difference

I COULD SAY that I was a well-adjusted and mild-tempered man. I'd row against the current, defying all logic, only when I had to—when there would be no alternative. Normally I'd consider each next step that I'd take as the logical outcome of the previous one, in the spirit of the old proverb *a man reaps what he sows*, and I'd be ready, more or less, to own up to my mistakes. On this day I would be faced with a temptation that I wasn't prepared for, and that seemed to have been preordained long before my time. It was true that the saying *everything happens for a reason* was not just some empty phrase. It turned out that Mr. Maslow's book hadn't appeared underneath my armpit by pure chance and that the architect of the high school hadn't placed Room 32 at the very beginning of the corridor purely by accident.

In my life, and especially in my childhood, I would often *quiver* in fear of one thing or another. The fears would be imaginary, such as fear of the dark or of thunder, but also real. When the immediate cause of my fear would go away, the grip of anxiety would slowly loosen and I would stop shaking. Soothed by soft voices or comforting touches of people who loved and cared for me, I'd push the fear aside and give in to dreams, to play, to love, or to whatever gave me pleasure. Nevertheless, there is a unique, life-changing quiver that stands out among all the others. When we feel it, we are changed forever. It resembles the red traffic light. It's a sign to stop . . . to listen and think. But it's far from easy to understand the restlessness we feel. When I saw Emilija Savić walking down the corridor, I first thought I was hallucinating; until then we'd mostly just met in her dreams. My astral body sprang to life—here I was, about to become involved in yet another supernatural story. I'd be a protagonist in an intriguing spiritual adventure in which some new mystery of life would be revealed. However, the clicking sound of her heels on the marble floor, the hubbub of students' voices behind the open door, and her verbal communication with a female student who handed her something all implied that Emilija Savić was actually there, *in the flesh.*

My astral body instantly retreated as my material body began to experience a strange physical reaction—I felt as if all the organs in my body were shaking to the point of being dislodged, which happened in a certain sense, since I could feel my heart practically *in my toes.* One of my kidneys ended up in my esophagus, my stomach was pulsating in my knees and my lungs, squeezed between the ribs, stopped breathing. My body was throbbing as one big bubbling cauldron, but despite all the mess inside, I still knew that the answer to the question *now what?* was hiding somewhere inside of me. Finding the answer would be a difficult task, considering the fact that my head resounded with a din resembling a heated argument among thousands of Bantu people in all their three hundred languages. For just a moment, a faint, hesitant thought managed to find its way through: what if Emilija Savić wasn't, in fact, a protagonist in this story in the first place? What if there was only one dreamer—me? In that case the story would be only mine, and Emilija Savić and I wouldn't have any *actual* affinity. It was a good thought, a true *lifesaver.* The question was whether I wanted to be saved in that way. Once we get entangled in our illusions and allow them to grow into us, letting them go becomes the hardest thing. The process of shedding our illusions is always a matter of *forced separation*, sad and hurtful, in which whole pieces of us get torn away and are lost forever.

Coming from my left, quietly and yet definitely, Room 32 appeared in my view with the self-confidence of a bare fact and saved me from the abyss. Instead of falling into the abyss, I fell through the door; I stumbled and almost ended up on my hands and knees. A venerable authority on all fours—wouldn't that be a sight to see. I tried to close the door several times, but something was impeding it, and I wasn't sure if it was the lock or if it was me being pulled backwards, out of the classroom, by some inexplicable force. Finally, I heard a *click!* and the closed door muffled the sound of heels continuing down the corridor.

If I'd succeeded in saving my reputation as a self-possessed man by not falling down, I didn't quite manage to keep it by my subsequent performance. Although intended as a confident presentation made by an experienced professional, my speech sounded more like inarticulate whining. I told them I hoped they would finish their studies and become designers whose works would impress the world, but I also mentioned that they could also wind up as interior designers, who were, in practice, just one step up from carpenters. I told them that finding a decently built structure with straight surfaces and right angles was a miracle nowadays, and got into a *don't get me started on all these builders that are considered professionals these days* kind of mood. And so on. At one point, I noticed that Maslow was *doing splits*, open upside down on the floor; the book was lying peacefully halfway between the teacher's desk and the door. I carefully picked up the book and, without closing it, laid it on the desk. The sun was shining on the open pages, and when I looked at them I saw exactly what I needed at that point. It was a perfect read for the occasion. I asked the best reader among them to volunteer to read the excerpt. "We don't do recitations," one of them said. "The drama school candidates are in the classroom next door," another added, and everyone started laughing. "If you take all the arts together, architecture is only one of them; eloquence is another. You should be able to understand this," I argued my case, but they didn't buy it. Still, after whispering briefly among themselves they chose one boy and he came to the place where I was standing to assume the role of the reader. Relieved, I listened to the boy reading while slowly pacing up and down the classroom. The boy seemed bright, had a clear voice and good diction, and I could picture him making an enviable oratorical performance of something as ordinary as a football game. Here, he was reading smart stuff that, theoretically, had the answers to all the questions that might arise from teenagers' jumbled minds. I listened carefully to the part about self-actualization, life as a continual process of making choices, the importance of listening to one's inner voice, taking responsibility, and being honest.

I refused to pay attention to the part that spoke unfavorably of illusions and developed strategies for their destruction. Turning to the wall, I saw three insects forming a peaceful triangle. There were two spiders and a winged ant, with some other sort of tiny insect that kept them company. I raised my hand towards them. I refused to believe that I did it with an intention to harm them—maybe I just wanted to check if they were alive and whether they'd react. Did I move too abruptly? I didn't know, but I felt that I was losing my footing and had to lean against the wall. The disturbed insects were trying to detach themselves from the surface of the wall, and the ones who managed to do so left tiny clouds of dust trailing in their wake. When I pulled my hand from the wall, I inadvertently threw an entire minuscule animal world into confusion and disorder. An invisible but sturdy construction of dust and spiderwebs was destroyed. Though tiny at first sight, the structure suddenly started expanding, and at one point it burst open, releasing thousands of agitated spiders and other small insects in a heavy cloud of dust. Overwhelmed with panic, I began throwing windows open. "Everybody out! Someone go and get some bug spray!" I screamed as I was trying to think of a solution for the impending disaster befalling the students as well as myself.

After the last student left the classroom, I was just about to leave too when I glimpsed a shadow in the corner of my eye. As if drawn by a strange kind of magnetism, with music in the background that was indescribable by any known onomatopoeic sound, I couldn't help but look. Was it possible? Sitting in the back row, the one beneath the coat hooks, the kind man that I'd met on the green plateau of the snow cliff was looking at me. I reacted with a silly, crooked smile on my face, one of those facial expressions that we unconsciously make when we realize that we've fallen victim to a practical joke. My head was already spinning and I was hesitating whether to leave the room or not; in short, I didn't know what to do with myself.

"Mr. Naumov!" my visitor said. "Forgive me for the exclamation mark, but I had to snap you out of the shock."

"Is it really *you*?" I replied in disbelief.

"Yes. Forgive me if I scared you."

"I'm not scared . . . rather astonished, really. Am I on *the other side*?"

"No, I am. I usually don't visit people unannounced, but . . . it couldn't have been otherwise this time. I had to intervene in the case of one of our protégées here. It turned out, however, that the situation was far more serious than I would have expected. You're affected as well."

"So, you know everything?" I asked him while straddling a chair right in front of the school desk he was sitting at. I leaned forward, placed my elbows on the same desk and, looking at him intently, waited.

"I know."

"And she, does she know?"

"She knows."

"You told her!!" If the two exclamation marks hadn't stopped me just at the right moment, I would have said the most awful things to him: *you squealing, manipulating, conniving*... However, I realized quickly that the anger that overwhelmed me was no more than the impulsive twitch of a man subdued, and that a holy man enveloped in such an aura of peacefulness was unassailable.

"Forgive me," I said. "You don't have to answer that."

"Listen to me, Petar: the two of you must talk. Neither of you can keep on living, hiding a secret like that. This is a small town, and you'll meet eventually. You're punishing yourselves, turning inevitability into a phobia, while, in fact, everything can be all right—imagine the joy of stealing a single conspiratorial glance at each other whenever you meet in the future. That will be enough. The relationship that you have is special and you were fortunate to experience it—would you really allow an act of God's grace to cause you pain, as if it were a curse? This thing that you two have is beyond this world and cannot harm others. It has nothing to do with your bodies, as you may well have realized by now. So you should both do everything in your power to make your physical encounters as rare as possible—they are just an obstacle for a relationship such as yours. However, when you do meet, let it be bearable for both parties. Still, for this to work, you two need to have a decent conversation. There! Maybe I've missed saying something, but you're a smart man... this will do."

"Is the distance between the two worlds really that great?" I asked.

"No, they're close. They intersect at various levels. The problem is not in the spatial distance between the two worlds. This weather doesn't agree with me... I'm leaving, I'm tired."

"Please, before you leave... I'd like to know your name."

"My name is Isaac. Isaac of Nineveh."

"The saint? From Syria?" I stared at him with my mouth wide open for a few moments, then I recovered my composure and continued the conversation with a dignified air. "But then you must be at least fourteen centuries old?"

"It doesn't show, does it?" he asked, his smiling face exhibiting playful arrogance.

"I wouldn't give you more than five," I said deadpan and quickly waved back to the hand that he raised in salute before leaving.

Chapter 18
Problems Encountered by the Emotionally Threadbare When Trying to Confess

"Hello, is this the Naumov household?"

"Yes, can I help you?"

There was no response across the void.

"You've reached the Naumovs, Anđelija speaking . . . Who are you looking for, ma'am?" she asked, with a chill feeling of suspicion clutching her throat.

There was no response, only the subdued sound of a suppressed gasp.

"Forgive me, this is a mistake." A woman's whisper crept into Anđa's ear.

"It's not a mistake, you've reached the right number." Anđa encouraged the conversation along with her last shreds of courage, unaware of the danger of getting herself into a game of *Russian roulette.*

"You're very kind, Mrs. Naumov. I know that I've reached the right number—the call is the mistake . . . Forgive me." The anonymous woman finished the conversation and hung up.

Anđa fell into a state of utter dismay. Her heart was pounding so hard that she thought it might jump out of her chest. Blood rushed to her head, and she mentally pictured herself riddled with tiny holes pouring out streams of blood to relieve the pressure that she was feeling now. Who was the woman looking for Petar? Where was he now? He'd left the house in the morning, and now it was already getting dark. "Dear God, what is happening to us?" Her loud rhetorical cry reached her husband who appeared framed in the doorway of their living room. He was standing there, with his face covered in dust and spiderwebs.

They looked like two desperate strangers, their encounter a mere accident. They were in emotional tatters. They wanted to exchange stories to clear the air, but they hesitated. Opening up proved more difficult than they could ever imagine—each had spent far too much time in their stuffy cocoon. They were now terrified of the troubles that a fresh confession could cause. Petar looked like a man who had returned home after long years living in a shabby attic—dirty and stained with soot and lime. Anđa was hopelessly and melodramatically afflicted by the whole thing. This steady and capable woman had moments in life when she didn't have the answer, but this was the first time she didn't even know the question. Their situation was no longer like any previous benign phase of their life—it was now absurd.

"Petar, a woman called. She was looking for you."

"What woman?" His startled eyes shot towards her.

"She didn't say," Anđa said as calmly as she possibly could.

"Did she say that she was looking for me?"

"Explicitly? No. Implicitly? Yes, since she obviously had nothing to say to me."

"Still, how do you know it was *me* that she wanted to talk to?"

"Well, her intention was to talk to somebody living here . . . ! Jesus, Petar, how many of us are there exactly in this apartment!?" Anđa asked in a shrill voice, losing all composure.

They were standing there, facing each other, a little closer than before. With their arms hanging heavily and their shoulders drooping, they were assessing each other with the eyes of exhausted animals.

"What is this? A suspicious wife throwing jealous fits?" Petar was the first to say something.

"Yes, it is."

"My dear wife, is it so hard for you to imagine that there is such a thing in the world as a relationship between a man and a woman that doesn't necessarily imply a physical reaction in their groin areas?"

"You mean a relationship with someone who is physically disabled?"

"Well, that does it. I'm afraid I am *not* defending myself on this one. No! I'm not talking about the physically disabled, I'm talking about healthy people."

"You're crazy. Completely crazy." The wife finally said it, establishing an amateur but, all symptoms taken into account, precise diagnosis of her husband's state.

"I'm not getting into any further discussion on this matter, Anđelija. Maybe I am crazy, but my conscience is clear. I'm not cheating on you . . . and that's it. Period."

"How can I be sure?"

"There's no other way but to believe me. Believe me . . . ! Fuck! Is it really so difficult?"

"I believe you," Anđa murmured in a conciliatory tone and with a strange look of determination in her eyes. She had already made up her mind, and there was no turning back now. A while back she had written down the names and numbers of several psychiatrists, just in case she ever needed them. Well, this was the moment.

Chapter 19
Looking for Meaning in an Unannounced Visit

ANĐELIJA NAUMOV'S STATE of mind couldn't be related in any way to that of Emilija Savić's life companion. What was more, Žarko had the benefit of a miraculous event that sparked a curious thriving of his creative powers. The revival of his spiritual being started when, completely out of nowhere, Erato, the Greek Muse of Lyric Poetry, paid him a visit. Mistakenly, no question about it, but that was how it took place. He had a pretty good idea of what happened—while they were sleeping, the mythical lady with the lyre surely wanted to lodge inspiration in Ema's head, but it was dark and his head and Ema's were resting peacefully next to each other, which must have been when the confusion took place.

The following night they were coming back from a literary soiree, organized on the occasion of a well-known local author's book launch. The author was a cynical and misogynist satirist, and they both loved his writing. Žarko greatly enjoyed reading books of that kind, perceiving them as a form of relaxation. For Ema, on the other hand, they had the allure of a Rubik's cube, but the puzzle she'd try to solve was not the same for her as for everyone else. She wasn't interested in making each side consist of stickers of the same color; she was driven by the complexity of the magic cube's inner structure, the internal pivot mechanism on which the entire puzzle rested. The same was true with this author's works—there was something on the pages of his books that she couldn't quite put her finger on, but she didn't trust him. She would twist the sentences, turn the lines upside down, uproot entire paragraphs, suspecting that, somewhere deep inside, the emotional magma of the author's being lay petrified, and that only by looking very closely could she perhaps glimpse the fears that gradually made the magma turn to stone. She never doubted that someone like him must be extremely sensitive, to the point of being absolutely terrified of anyone ever seeing him *whimper*, which would ruin forever his macho image.

That's what Ema was thinking about—first out loud, and then inwardly, in her mind. They were walking holding hands, when all of a sudden . . . all sorts of words and concepts started swarming in Žarko's head. Ema's wet and cold palm was telling him something; he could tell that his beloved Ema was overcome with restlessness again. A thought came to his mind about *the wind* and its role in all that, then *the ice* . . . then *dejection* . . . some *bees* were there too . . . where there are bees, there's always, naturally, *honey*. And so forth, although he still wasn't sure what it all meant.

He said nothing to Ema. In vain did his clients come to look for him in his office the next day. They called his landline and mobile phone, but without success, and when the same thing happened the following day, the resentful clients were on the brink of lodging a complaint to the Lawyer's Association against this particular member.

Meanwhile, behind the closed door with all his phones turned off, the newborn poet was working diligently. Žarko's profession had crippled his verbal expression so much that he always seemed unable to go beyond the limits of the rhetoric and legal terminology that he normally used, but now he was experiencing sheer joy while hordes of fluttery adjectives, miraculous metaphors, and impossible semantic combinations invaded his mind. Not that everything went smoothly. The table was littered with sheets of paper torn from the writing pad. He'd write something, then he'd cross it out, tear the paper, crumple it, and throw it away. He had one coffee after another, until eventually he ran out of clean cups. He postponed a bottle of Gorki List till later, when he'd finished his poem; that poem would get finished, so help him God. He lined up the words, then rearranged them . . . and there it was, the first rhyme was born. Bravo, poet! He'd give himself support and praise every now and again. He'd been aware that there was such a thing as creative madness, and he seemed to have fallen victim to its power, quite by chance . . . but, man, didn't he feel *swell*.

Žarko's fit of creative productivity lasted for two working days, and everything *came out* just right: poetry from the pen, Gorki List from the bottle, and a drunken poet into the street.

Chapter 20
The Assertion That *No Poet Ever Wrote about His Own Wife's Eyes* Refuted

THERE'S NOTHING EASIER than to give clever advice when someone else's life is at stake, I thought, reproaching Isaac of Nineveh, my spiritual guide and mentor. Still, I knew that I was pathetically trying to find someone else to blame.

I didn't plan on calling the Naumovs and suddenly not knowing what to say. I never thought I would actually call in the first place; I didn't think I'd have the nerve to go through with it. But all the way home from school and for quite some time afterwards all I could hear in my head was a persistent voice picking at my brain, saying *you have to talk . . . ! you have to talk . . . ! you have to talk . . . !* at a rate of a hundred times a minute. If Petar and I really had to talk, and it seemed that there was no avoiding it, I decided to approach the problem as a calm, cool-headed person would. I was going to make the first move; since I was the one who started it, I should be the one to get us out of this mess. Like a robot, a being devoid of any kind of emotion, I picked up the phone and pressed the six digits. I didn't think about anything while I waited for someone to answer—it was like I was calling a taxi or ordering food. But then, when Anđelija Naumov's *hello* reached me across the void, I couldn't believe my ears. I felt as if I'd just fallen victim to an awful setup; all of a sudden I became acutely aware of how scared I was, how wrong it all felt, and how unable I was to say anything.

The moment I heard Anđelija Naumov's voice, I experienced the entropic forces doing their thing—I suffered a shameful moral diminution into a thing smaller than an average poppy seed. Anđelija Naumov, unlike me, had the strength of a Penelope, known and praised in poetry as the epitome of the faithful wife. There was only one difference: this was not a Greek tragedy in which everybody suffers and no one is to blame. There was only one person to blame here, and her name was Emilija Savić.

I wasn't capable of telling the truth, and I wasn't capable of saying anything else. I kept silent, *dodging* Anđelija's questions, postponing the beginning of the conversation, pretending it was a mistake; and then, without introducing myself, I hung up, hiding myself in the sound of the phone disconnecting—a perfect example of masochism at work. I spent considerable time in dejected self-examination after that call. My determined attempts at reconciling the two worlds I inhabited proved to be futile. All the noble, otherworldly ideals that I so passionately believed in were still there, but—was I deluding myself in trying to abide by them in reality?

I would have probably spent hours more dissecting my spiritual and emotional being had Žarko not appeared at the door in a novel and unprecedented condition. He stood there before me with his tie loosened and his shirt collar pulled open, with his hair ruffled and half-wet, with his eyes full of some strange rapture, and . . . there was no mistake about it, he was a little drunk. After the telephone ordeal that I'd just gone through, this came as a blessed relief.

"Well, now. What's with this new look, *my handsome young man?*" I couldn't stop smiling.

"No sarcasm, please. I'd like to ask for your undivided attention, worthy of the moment that is to follow. Miss Ema, a poet is standing before you."

"A real one?" I could barely restrain myself from bursting

out laughing.

"As real as it gets. I wrote a poem," Žarko said importantly with a light nod.

"You wrote a poem?"

"I did . . . for you. Listen," he issued the most tender of commands and began reciting:

THE TWO OF US WALKING
The two of us walking hand in hand,
Looking as happy as can be;
But your cold palm tells another story
We're keeping our distance . . . or aren't we?

I can tell whenever you are restless
But I let winds blow my worries away
For it's too early for us to feel sorrow
Love's what I wish for! Without delay.

I don't push my luck—I ask no questions,
Unsure and pained, I just keep quiet
Hoping that, maybe, I could be wrong . . .
That it's just a figment of my imagination
Whenever you seem to be so silent.

Please know that my heart burns with fire
That will easily thaw all your fears away
Let tears of sorrow trickle down your cheek
And soon happiness will come your way.

And behold, already I feel your palm burn
With peacefulness that disperses your fears,
And yet it's just one of many battles
That our love must fight over many years.

What could I have possibly said to this . . . !? What indeed?

Chapter 21
Spiritus Realis

IF THERE IS anything that can bear testament to the existence of spiritual reality, the story that is about to be told could be it. The plot unfolds in a dark and dreary, somewhat Van Gogh-like setting; as for the time in which the story is set, that is unknown, but judging by the torches and candles used as lighting, it must be ancient history.

I lived in a house of the simplest rectangular shape, with a single entrance at the very beginning of a long wall. There were eight rooms, one after the other, and in order to enter a certain room one would have to pass through all the preceding ones. My room was the third in the row, which meant that the number of people disturbed by my going back and forth was fewer than the number of the people who'd pass through my private space several times a day. There was only one man who'd do it not more than twice a day—in the morning when he'd leave the house, which didn't bother me since I was usually asleep then, and late in the evening, when he returned. He'd pass with his shoulders slouched and his head down, so I never saw his face. He'd murmur something and then, looking as if he was uncomfortable or sorry about something, just disappear in the dimness of the next room as lightly as he could, like a ghost. Nobody knew what he did or where he spent his time; rumor had it that he was a former convict and that he'd served a long sentence possibly linked to a violent crime, maybe even murder. In any case, I wasn't afraid of him; I stayed out of his way, respecting his need for privacy and his apparent desire to remain anonymous.

That night, not five minutes had passed since he walked through my room, before he came back. This time he wasn't just passing—he'd come to see me. Distressed, as if frightened by something, he was wringing his arms and asking for help:

"It's burning again . . . He lit it again, he must be up to something. You know, like the other night. You helped me then—would you help me again? Please?"

The man was shaking. What was I supposed to tell him? I couldn't recall him ever approaching me before, nor could I think of any *burning* incident in the area.

"Again, you say . . . Well, let's have a look." And so we went. My acceptance made him far more cheerful. He led the way briskly, taking me to his room which was at the very end, the last room of this unusual building.

We went inside an entirely empty room. The only source of light, coming from the window, was some kind of amber glow that interrupted the darkness pervading the room. I searched for the source of the unusual light that disconcerted the man and, looking towards the window, I noticed that it was coming from something that looked like a sunroof on a house opposite ours about ten meters away. I didn't feel like getting into what it could be—whether it was the laboratory of a physicist, a mere reflection of some shiny object, or something of the sort. I didn't see the danger that scared the poor man so much, but I had to do something to relieve his fear, so I opened the window. I was just about to call out to whomever was there, when the room was plunged into darkness. There was nothing but dead silence around us. Everything became clear to me—the source of the poor man's fear was in his own room, and not outside. I wasn't curious enough to find out what exactly the object was that stood in the left corner of his room and reflected the strange light in the window glass, nor did I feel like explaining. I said good-bye to my unusual, now *safe* host, leaving him in his state of blissful ignorance.

I was coming back down a long, narrow hall, a passage whose existence I'd been unaware of before. Although without a single source of light, the passage still seemed to be in twilight, and the visibility inside was sufficient. It was an empty space without any doors, probably linking two pavilions. On the other side of the passage there was a building with the same layout as the one I lived in, with rooms lined up one after the other, but I was walking down the narrow, stone-paved passage without any idea how I was going to find my way out. All of a sudden, coming from my right, I heard the loud sound of a wall being pulled down. I saw a piece of the wall falling on the opposite side. A passage to one of the rooms gaped open in front of me, and I could tell by my present position that it must be the fourth room in the row of the adjoining structure. I didn't feel for a second that I shouldn't go in. It was clear that the passage had opened *for me*.

I stepped into yet another dark room, lit by only one candle. There was a woman sitting at a table with her chin cupped in her palms. With her head bent forward and a heavy chunk of hair hiding her face, I couldn't see who she was. She gave a start at the sound of my footsteps, then raised her eyes and brushed her hair back with her hand. I could see her face now. Emilija Savić stepped forward and came up to me.

"Welcome, Petar," she said smiling.

I recognized true affection in that smile. Unrestrained joy immediately filled the whole space. She approached me, took me by the hands, and led me to the table, never for once taking her eyes off me. Time can be a loose category, depending on what it is filled with, so I couldn't tell exactly how long we looked each other in the eyes without saying a word. We didn't decide to remain silent—the words that were to be said between us simply *knew*: words know when to be said, they also know when to be quiet or not turn up at all because . . . some things are clear even without words.

"Is this real?" I asked and looked at her for the answer as the candlelight flickered on her face.

"Yes, I think. Can you feel this?" She scratched her nails lightly down my hand.

"Yes, although it doesn't hurt."

"I didn't mean to hurt you."

"No, not that . . . ! This encounter doesn't hurt," I said.

"It was not meant to hurt. This meeting is necessary for us to exchange the knowledge—although our knowledge is the same. Am I right? Do you understand our relationship? What we mean to each other?"

"We're a perfect couple of astral bodies. Our physical connection is nonexistent, or, at least, is not perceivable by the senses," I said readily, without much thinking.

"In other words, we're two paranormal beings in a normal world—*spiritus realis* as a way of life. Yes . . . that's the right definition," Ema agreed, all the while staring gravely at the bottom of my nose.

We were silent again, looking intently at the flame of the candle. I pinched my fingers to quench the flame and crushed the blackened end of the wick. It was me again who interrupted the silence:

"Ema, correct me if I'm wrong, but your dreams must be a reflection of your inner turmoil?"

"Yes. They definitely are. I think too much—like Martha, Mary's sister, when Jesus Christ reprimands her for not being at peace with herself. That's me—overcome with disquiet, with a restless mind and a passionate heart. Here I am, celebrating individuality and yet I'm afraid of living a lonely life . . . How would you define taste, Petar?" she suddenly asked, changing the subject.

"It is one of the characteristics of a man's authentic makeup,"

I replied, caught off guard again. I couldn't explain the nervousness that I felt when she was obviously talking to me as if she was talking to her other *self*.

"That's it, that's exactly it! I knew you would understand, Petar. And it hurt so much when, first, I came to realize how distant two people can be, and again, when I had to come to terms with it. All those incompatibilities pained me—seeing people silence the music that speaks directly to the heart, or turn some poet's *blood and guts* into paper cones and painter's hats."

"Slow down, Ema, take it easy."

"I know, I know," she whispered. We were whispering the whole time, as if we were being spied upon or hunted, and we weren't—we met in a time that was out of everyone's reach.

"You have your imagination, the world of abstraction, the universe. Don't dwell on ephemeral things," I was trying to comfort her.

"I try not to, but sometimes I simply can't help myself wanting things that cannot be. Fortunately, our minds can make everything possible . . . even the things that cannot be."

"For example?" I encouraged her.

"Our minds can go beyond perverted truths promoted into dogmas, beyond stupid canons established by God knows whom . . . They can go where I can't even begin to think to *set foot*. Mount Athos is the best example. And I've been there."

"You couldn't have been," I said in disbelief.

"Oh, I was, in spirit. Perhaps it was defiance on my part, but also strong conviction. In my view, there is no justification for the fact that no woman can set foot in any of the monasteries of Mount Athos. Christ has nothing to do with that idiocy. In any case, the most important places are never reached by crossing physical distances. Not even on earth."

"Such rules must have started out as big misunderstandings and then ended up as conventions."

"I know that you understand. You know everything even

without asking. Your eyes are open wide and you see things fully and clearly. The problem, the solution, the cause, the effect, destiny itself—in the wider context, it's all connected and it makes sense. We complain about the constraints we encounter in the course of our earthly existence—about our family or some of its members, about our colleagues and the neighbor next door, and we must know that complaining is out of place. When everything passes and life starts coming to an end, everyone realizes that their surroundings have been exactly the way they should have been so that they would become what they should have become."

"I was just about to say the same thing, Ema. Didn't we say at the beginning that those like us don't need any words to communicate? And look at us now, almost interrupting each other, fighting like hungry lions over who gets to speak first."

"Forgive me . . . I just had to analyze the *big picture*."

"All right. How can you tell the peacefulness of a wise man from the peacefulness of an indifferent man?" I asked.

"You're not indifferent!!!" The three exclamation marks lashed me like the cord of a horse whip. "An indifferent man," she continued, considerably thrown off balance, "would never bother to rush to the edge of a steep, snowy precipice from which, if he fell, he'd fall into nothingness . . . just to save me. An indifferent man's path would never lead him into a cave whose exit is narrower than his shoulders."

"I didn't say I was indifferent, although there are so many things that I still don't know about myself. I've discovered certain things about my life only recently, the things I never knew existed . . . It's happened all at once. I'm confused. And it's all thanks to you, Miss Emilija Savić. Now I know that we're on the same path of life. We're on the same front, where universal values fight for recognition."

"Yes—compassion, goodness, beauty, love . . . love before all. But tell me, my dearest soul mate, what happens when the universal takes over your entire being but your existence is still inextricably bound to reality? Let me give you an example, first-hand. Every inch of my reality is heavily suffused with the spiritual, and it shows. Only few can understand it, and as for the rest—they just think I'm crazy. Spirituality is something to be hidden from people, or else one is threatened with *excommuni-cation* from the real world."

"Beauty, love . . . You go on and on about the same things, Ema. What about evil? Can you see it anywhere?"

"I believe in natural beauty and natural goodness. I don't believe that things are evil by nature. But when they are evil, there is always goodness residing at the borders of evil. They're back-to-back; extremes intrigue me. I'm fascinated by the mixture of splendor and misery, of an image that is at the same time horrible and appealing. That's why I love the film *Dead Man Walking*. If you can imagine—a well-meaning woman and a monstrous killer awaiting execution. She's the most powerful being in the whole world, whereas he's the most miserable one. I speak in general terms—love has all the power, while hate is nothing but destruction. I'm weak, Petar. I'm just a larva in a cocoon, maybe a butterfly one day. I'm not a healer—one dirty look is enough to shatter me completely. And I'm egotistical as well! For my own safety, I'd impose a ban on giving dirty looks . . . although my egoism would surely bring benefit to all. I wish everyone could celebrate life as it is, with joy in their eyes, in the Name of the One that shall come . . . that must come, otherwise this story would have no meaning. I refuse to believe that things are meaningless!!!"

I didn't know what to say.

"From time to time I have this insane thought that I could take a killer in my arms, so that I could feel that he was alive, that he was human. If he wanted to hear me out, I'd tell him . . ."

"What would you tell him? Do you think you would manage to tell him anything before the blade of his cold heart pierces yours and lets you bleed to death?"

"I believe in miracles, Petar. You're a miracle! This encounter is a miracle . . . ! I've lived to experience miracles—" Looking towards an hourglass placed at the window, Ema failed to finish the sentence. She got up from the chair. "Time is running out, Petar. You have to go. This passage only opens once in a hundred years."

"Will we see each other again, Ema?"

"Not like this. We don't need it. Now we know."

"We do."

"I love that you exist, Petar Naumov."

"This way of existing would have been impossible without you."

She said good-bye the same way she greeted me. She walked with me to the wall holding both of my hands. I passed proudly through the opening, feeling as if I'd just been crowned, and turned left, deciding to take my leave quickly.

Chapter 22
A Possible Epilogue (Based on a Subjective Judgment of an Ephemeral Passer-By and Thus Not Corroborated by Emilija Savić's and Petar Naumov's Notes)

Facsimile of Petar Naumov's manuscript

THE RATHER ILLEGIBLE notes that Petar Naumov left made it impossible to conclude, even when reading through to the very last line, whether the critical encounter between him and Emilija Savić had happened in his dream or in Emilija Savić's dream, and whether or not the mysterious man had played any major role in it. Petar didn't seem to consider this very important. What became quite evident, however, even to the naked eye, was the fact that the encounter proved to be completely advantageous for all the protagonists of this extraordinary story.

Everything fell into place. Petar didn't end up in a psychiatric ward after all, since all the impediments he'd encountered from the first moment he'd found himself in Ema's dream had now been removed. Anđa, soothed by the reestablished harmony of her marriage, easily swallowed the lump in her throat that had been stuck there for more than a month. Ema was also able to breathe freely again, since she didn't have a guilty conscience anymore. Žarko basked in poetic glory, feeling more than grateful for the past emotional tension and thankful to the lyrical muse that, by pure chance, came his way.

Here they were, all four of them, in the luxurious reception hall of the best hotel in town. They were attending yet another wedding ceremony. They didn't sit at the same table, but it happened that they exchanged greetings twice—first in the commotion when the bride and the groom exchanged their *until death do us part* vows before the registrar, and then when they were leaving, in the parking lot in front of the hotel. Neither Petar nor Ema were exceptionally happy about greeting each other, given that the degree of intimacy they felt was in inverse proportion to the physical distance between them, but there was no escaping it—so, they were going to do it right. A short parade of civil words and good wishes was furled out. Everyone shook hands with everyone—Žarko and Petar, Anđa and Žarko, Ema and Anđa, and then finally the two of them. *All the best, Ema. Good night, Petar.* Hand went to hand in a polite grasp, exhibiting an admirable detachment.

Jovanka Živanović was born in 1959 in Teočin-Gornji Milanovac municipality, Serbia. She graduated from the Faculty of Economics in Kragujevac. She lives in Cacak. *Fragile Travelers* is her first work translated into English.

Jovanka Kalaba is a graduate student at the University of Belgrade in the department of Philology. This is her first book-length translation published in English.

Sketching Women

LEARN TO DRAW LIFELIKE FEMALE FIGURES
A CROQUIS COURSE FOR BEGINNERS

Atelier 21

Edited by
Tsubura Kadomaru

TUTTLE Publishing
Tokyo | Rutland, Vermont | Singapore

Table of Contents